The Tanglewood Desperadoes

There was a saying about Southern Colorado's Tanglewood: once you entered you could never find your way out.

A savage and broken landscape, Tanglewood was the perfect place to hide from the law since no man carrying a badge ever entered it, preferring the Tanglewood to do his work for him. So when Trace Dawson and his gang rode in, they were men without hope. Crooked land-pirates had taken their land and their homes from them. Now they were planning to fight back, whatever that might involve. . . .

The Tanglewood Desperadoes

Logan Winters

A Black Horse Western

ROBERT HALE · LONDON

© Logan Winters 2010
First published in Great Britain 2011

ISBN 978-0-7090-9043-4

Robert Hale Limited
Clerkenwell House
Clerkenwell Green
London EC1R 0HT

www.halebooks.com

Typeset by
Derek Doyle & Associates, Shaw Heath
Printed and bound in Great Britain by
CPI Antony Rowe, Chippenham and Eastbourne

CHAPTER ONE

Above the Tanglewood a three-quarter silver moon floated, surrounded and partly concealed by ghostly wisps of high cloud. Dan Sumner sat hunched in the copse of blackthorn, willow brush and scrub oak that proliferated in this southern section of Colorado. All of the night sounds were familiar to him. Coyotes lurking, the heavy beat of a low-flying horned owl's wings, peeper frogs performing their nightly rituals, the gasps of bullfrogs along the stream which meandered across the Tanglewood, the occasional slithering sound of a harmless bull snake.

The wind shifted, grew cooler, and Dan Sumner drew his coat collar up, wishing on this one night that he were not alone. But he was; even Johnny Johnson, the kid who seemed to fit his name somehow, unremarkable, and forgettable, had gone off toward Lordsberg to settle scores with Storm Ross and Prince Blakely. Dan had not gone because he had made his try the day before and had gotten himself shot in the leg for his efforts.

Now swollen and fiery, his leg throbbed and caused him to throw back his head and collapse on his blankets to stare up at the drifting moon through the tangle of underbrush. A small creature, probably a kangaroo rat, crossed his chest, and Dan swatted at it in annoyance.

It was hard for a man to find peace.

Dan was beginning to hate the Tanglewood. He had begun to question his own good sense as he lay hunted, pursued and wounded in the vast array of broken canyons, ravines, twisted trails, and teeming vegetation of the Tanglewood. Here there were thickets of raspberries with almost inedible fruit, cane and mesquite, stunted pinyon pines, sumac, manzanita, blackthorn and scrub-oak trees all jumbled together in some nearly impassable tangle that Nature seemed to have formed as a joke or as a challenge to men. If you didn't get stuck on a thorn or bitten by some small creature each day, you knew you were not in the Tanglewood.

On a few, occasional perfect mornings Dan Sumner had risen from his bed to appreciate the mysterious, primitive beauty of the Tanglewood. There was the silver-bright stream rushing down from the canyon head, the spray of color where the blue gentian and foxglove flourished along the banks of the stream, along with the lupine and black-eyed Susans across the scattered grassy parks.

But those days were rare. Tanglewood was a prison to those who sought refuge there. It was usually too hot in the day, too frigid at night, crawling with uninvited animal guests, neither edible nor friendly. Bobcats had a large community there. Badgers were not uncommon, nor were raccoons. Nor angry-tempered black bears and the occasional puma. Diamondback rattlesnakes were concealed under every flat rock.

All animals best enjoyed by viewing them in illustrated books.

They weren't comforting to live with.

As for the pretty flowers, well, they were only an occasional sight as well. More common were the barren coils of raspberry vines, the sting of nettles, the thickets of nopal cactus, clumps of catclaw and cholla, or 'jumping cactus', ready to snag any passer-by with their silver barbs.

Along the creek there were treacherous bogs, clotted with cattails and dead reeds. The stench that rose from this rotting vegetation rivaled that of any black tupelo swamp in Dan's home state of Mississippi. And Lord help you if you took the notion to try crossing one of these sinkhole areas. It wasn't drowning a man would face, but a smothering death in the fetid ooze as it sucked him down. No one could save a man foolish enough to venture into the bogs.

Tanglewood Canyon was a mecca for the small things: chiggers, mites, fire ants, gnats, deer flies and mosquitoes. A few larger insect-types, such as scorpions, centipedes and tarantulas made it not advisable, but imperative, that you shook out your boots every morning before putting them on or suffer the painful consequences. Up along the high ridge, dwelling in small caves, there were clusters of brown bats which came out every evening, swarming to dart along the stream, looking for the smaller insects to devour, and in the daytime there was the cheerful presence of buzzards who seemed to have no trouble finding carrion in the Tanglewood – some of it human remains.

The Tanglewood was not a place lawmen entered willingly. They had more sense, apparently, than the outlaws who sheltered there. The law seemed to be saying, 'Let them go. Tanglewood will take care of them soon enough.'

Dan sat up, scratching at his head. Something had gotten into his hair. He wanted to make a break for it. However, Lordsberg, where he was a wanted man, was to the east. To the west was the imposing bulk of the Rocky Mountains. To the south the land was open desert nearly all the way to the Mexican border. But that meant a trek of hundreds of miles across a waterless flat desert. Anyone looking for him would catch up with him quickly if he did not die along the way.

No, for now all he could do was continue to hole up in the Tanglewood, and hope the other boys had some luck. Having no real option, Dan sat up again with pained impatience, clutching his injured right leg as the mocking night moon drifted past the Tanglewood. Perhaps morning would bring some solution.

Trace Dawson led his small band of men along the dark back alleyways of Lordsberg, again wondering how things had gotten this far. So that life became a kill-or-be-killed proposition with the other side holding most of the guns. The men of the Tanglewood did not speak as they rode, not even sharing a whisper. Johnny Johnson on his little paint pony rode solemnly as he kept pace with Trace. His young face was as grim as a pallbearer's. Perhaps it was an apt expression. They had likely planned their own funerals in returning to Lordsberg. And it would no longer be a secret to the town that this was what they had in mind. Dan Sumner had tipped them off yesterday when he had the desperate urge to visit his girlfriend, Kate.

Trace reflected that that was one of the things a man had always to take into account when dealing with youngsters. They were prone to dangerous impulses.

The night was still, the silver three-quarter moon suspended in the silence, but from across town they could hear the tinkly sounds of a piano from one of the three saloons. The Wabash, probably. Trace couldn't remember either of the others having such a contraption. But then, he had been gone awhile and had never been much of a saloon-goer. They were places where men went to brag, get stupid, risk a fight and throw their money away. Trace Dawson was no Puritan, but the whole concept seemed pointless to him.

They reined their horses up in the stillness of the night. Trace, Johnson, Curt Wagner and Torrance. The bank was just ahead, and although they doubted that it would be guarded at this time of night, still Dan Sumner's rash visit to town might have alerted Lordsberg.

Trace waited patiently, his big gray horse shifting its feet uneasily under him. How had they come to this?

He had his theories, of course. The West was no longer the sole domain of Western men. Trace thought the railroad was to blame for this. Where men like his kind had fought through bands of Indians and forced their way west, now it seemed that anyone with the price of a ticket or who was simply capable of hopping a freight was flooding into the new frontier towns. They did not know the ways of the West and couldn't be bothered to learn them. They brought their Eastern ways, Eastern sensibilities with them, not understanding the Red Man, the wild country, survival on the plains. What they thought they knew of the West was that there was no code of ethics, that you were free to shoot a man down if you didn't care for him or he was giving you an argument, that everything they came upon was there for the taking. It was like watching honor fade before his eyes. The vigor had gone from the land, but not the violence nor the greed.

The newcomers had no understanding of the old West where a man lived by a solemn, unwritten, but inflexible code. You treated every man with respect until he proved himself to be your enemy. You did not lie, steal, poach, murder, back-shoot a man, or molest a woman. There was a long list of laws, not scribbled down anywhere, but as firmly etched in each of the old-time Westerners' minds as if they had been inscribed in stone.

But the new breed had come, viewing the West as a vast arena for rapaciousness, where there was no law and no moral restraints.

They had left their Bibles at home.

There was no telling what they wrote to their friends and family back home about how they were carving out a new life in the West, but the truth was they had simply come in with money and guns and had begun system-atically robbing the early settlers and driving them off their land. Dan Sumner had been just a young kid trying to get his dirt farm started, hoping to make enough out of his patch to ask Kate Cousins to marry him. Johnny Johnson, even younger, had saved his wages from his cattle-herding days and thrown up a small cabin along the Wakapee River and finally managed to bring in some blooded horses to raise. There were only eight animals in his small herd, but he had hopes. Trace Dawson had bartered with the Ute Indians for ownership of a pocket valley south of the Wakapee and he had begun raising a herd of sleek cattle, most of them now shorthorn stock.

Ben Torrance had almost no land, but he had found a way to get by after striking water on his few acres of dry land. An entire summer he had dug with pick and shovel until he found water in his deep well which now served most of the poor, thrown-together town of Lordsberg.

The money men had come with their land claims signed by some bureaucrats two thousand miles away in Washington DC through bribery or corruption. The kind of men who had never had a shovel or a rope in their hands in their entire lives, and likely would not know what to do with either.

What it was, was legal thievery.

Curt Wagner had been a drifting man and tired of that way of life. Lordsberg had by almost unanimous consent hired him on as a sort of lawman – there were a few drunks and derelicts already attracted by

Lordsberg's first saloon, the Wabash, started by Kate's father, Gentry Cousins who knew that there was always money to be made in rough country if there was a whiskey barrel handy.

Gentry hadn't liked the manners of some of the incomers, especially when his daughter was serving bar, and he had asked Curt to take care of matters. And he had. For a while, but soon there were too many to handle. Men brought in by Blakely, Storm Ross and the others who had laid claim to everything the old-country-men had built up. Of course the old breed of men had no legal title to their claims. There was no such thing in the early years. A man found a place of his own, settled there and started building for his future and for his sons and daughters. Storm Ross and Prince Blakely knew this, of course, and they had maneuvered in the capital for possession of the Wakapee Valley.

And gotten it.

Almost all of the original settlers were now dispossessed. Gentry Cousins had managed to keep his saloon, the Wabash, but he couldn't pour enough whiskey to keep all of the roughnecks working for Blakely and Ross happy and two new saloons had sprung up almost overnight – the Black Panther and the Golden Eagle.

Curt Wagner had tried to keep order in the town, but order wasn't what the Blakely-Ross group wanted, and they had called an election to oust him. There were so many hired thugs on the other side that the original pioneers had no chance. A lot of them were roughed-up at the polling places. Curt had been stripped of his badge and a new town marshal, Kaylin Standish, installed.

A few of the evicted land-holders had objected vigorously to the way they were being treated. Ben Torrance had gotten into a gunfight with a host of Standish's deputies and wounded two of them before he was driven off his property. Johnny Johnson had stood up to complain at what was supposedly a town council meeting, but had been called only to solidify the Blakely-Ross group's effective stranglehold on the territory. Johnson had been beaten as he left the council chambers.

Each of them had been outlawed for causes such as resisting arrest, refusing to obey a lawful order and squatting on illegally-occupied land. What law there was in Lordsberg – the law of Blakely-Ross – had driven them off. Banished them to the Tanglewood.

They had gathered together, angrily plotting and swearing vengeance.

On this night their time had come. The time had come to take back the town.

There weren't enough of them to accomplish this by main force, though Johnson and Curt Wagner still nurtured enough recent anger to make them vote for that suicidal plan. Trace Dawson had a different idea. He had suggested it as they gathered around a campfire in the Tanglewood.

'We've got to see that the venture doesn't profit Blakely or Storm Ross. When they start losing money, they'll pull up stakes and take their roughnecks with them. After all, they're only here for the profit.'

They had then discussed various ways of making the Lordsberg investment useless to Ross and Blakely. There were a few odd ideas proposed and some that were quite practical. The one they had all agreed on was designed to pull the capital out from under the land-vultures – they wouldn't get far without money to pay their gang of thugs.

So on this night with the silver moon riding high, Trace Dawson and his band of men had set off to clean out the Lordsberg bank.

The frame building sat near the center of town, but was set off a little on a side street. They had discussed trying it by daylight, but Trace thought it better if they were not all identifiable. They were well known in the area, and although they could wear masks, their horses could not be similarly disguised. Besides, there was a greater chance of a shoot-out in the daytime.

Curt Wagner, who seemed to have some experience with such matters in his background, had taken a look at the bank vault a few days earlier and returned calling it 'nothing but a glorified pillbox.' He was sure he could crack it even by moonlight. So they had decided to ride with the rising moon. Perhaps it was not a wise decision, but these were desperate men and emptying out the bank would strike a sudden, piercing thrust into the heart of the Blakely-Ross organization.

Trace saw no one along the street, but that did not mean they were not there. Besides, the town marshal, Kaylin Standish must have had some system for routinely patrolling there. There hadn't been time to learn Standish's usual pattern; that would have meant some of them having to sneak around Lordsberg where they could have been instantly recognized and locked up.

They swung down from their horses beside the bank, in the alley that separated it from a saddlery. Trace, Curt Wagner and Ben Torrance made their way to the front of the bank leaving Johnny Johnson to hold the horses and keep watch.

The lock on the front door which had a formidable appearance was quickly opened by Wagner's nimble fingers and they entered the darkness of the bank lobby.

'Open those roller-shades,' Trace said and Ben Torrance stepped to the black window shades, letting them roll up. Immediately the dark room was flooded with silver moonlight.

'Perfect,' Curt Wagner said, and he rubbed his hands together in anticipation as he stepped toward the bank vault.

'Better keep an eye out, Ben,' Trace told Torrance. Someone with a keen eye might notice that the blinds were up, although a casual passerby, if he were concerned enough to glance that way would probably assume that someone had neglected to draw the blinds that day.

'Can you see?' Trace asked Curt as the tall man peered at the locks of the safe.

'If you'll move your shadow,' Wagner answered with a touch of irritation. Trace quickly moved aside and left Wagner to his task.

'Someone's moving out there,' Ben Torrance hissed, and Trace went to the window where the sad-faced

15

Torrance half-crouched looking out at the moonlit street.

'Where? I don't see anybody?'

'Up the street. Near the corner of the dry goods store. No, I don't see him now,' Torrance said, wiping at his forehead nervously.

'Keep watching. It's early for the saloons to be closing and late for the stores to be open. Shouldn't be many people around.'

'Except Standish and his deputies,' Ben Torrance said. The small, balding man was jittery, unhappy with his role in the robbery. Originally the plan had been to leave Torrance in their camp and bring Dan Sumner with them to the bank, but Sumner's love life had ruined that plan.

Kaylin Standish had spotted Dan loitering around the Wabash Saloon, hoping to meet with Kate Cousins, and had opened up with his revolver, tagging Dan's leg. Trace placed a hand briefly on the nervous Ben Torrance's shoulder and then turned back to watch Curt Wagner at work.

There wasn't much to see. Wagner had already opened the so-called pillbox. He stood grinning at Trace, his teeth bright in the moonlight.

'I told you,' Curt said.

'Get everything out of there except the silver money. 'Deeds, titles, legal documents. I mean to cripple Prince Blakely and Ross.'

Curt Wagner was already at it, shoving currency and documents – everything from mortgages to title papers – into the burlap bags they had brought for that purpose. Trace helped out, moving as rapidly as he could. They didn't take a moment to glance at what they took, they just shoved it into their sacks.

Curt said, 'There won't even be anyone legally married in Lordsberg; do we want all these courthouse papers, Trace?'

'Everything we can carry. Gold and currency first, then everything else that will snarl up the works.'

'Hurry up!' Ben Torrance urged them from the window where he still stood guard shakily.

It didn't take them more than five minutes, since they stole at random and didn't take the time to examine what they were taking. Crossing to the door, Trace told Ben:

'You'd better go out first. We've got both hands filled with loot.'

Ben Torrance made a small miserable sound as he stepped through the door into the cool of night, gun in hand. Curt Wagner and Trace were right on his heels, lugging the stuffed burlap bags. Ten paces to the alley-way. Secure the sacks and off into the Tanglewood.

That's what they all were thinking when the guns opened up in the night.

CHAPTER TWO

The first shot, fired by a man with a handgun from the alleyway across the street struck Trace Dawson's bootheel as he was swinging aboard his gray gelding. The solid impact of lead against leather was enough to twist him around, driving him off balance. And it sent a shiver up along his leg to the survival center in his brain: *Get out of here!*

He managed to half-mount and start the gray from a full stop into a dead run, clinging to the side of the saddle as other shots rang out around him. Trace had no chance of firing back with one hand hanging precariously on the pommel, the other filled with a sack of bank loot.

Someone among them did manage to get off three answering shots. Trace thought it likely that it had been young Johnny Johnson since he had been unencumbered by the spoils they carried. It made no difference. Trace's big horse cleared the head of the alley in no time at all, taking the turn toward the west, effectively cutting off any possible sight lines the ambushers might have had.

Only now as he pounded down the main street past the few startled citizens did Trace manage to drag himself fully upright on to the saddle. Glancing across his shoulder he saw that all of his crew had made it safely. Johnny Johnson was in the lead with Curt Wagner and Ben Torrance, hatless now, close on his horse's heels. He could not determine if any of them were wounded though Curt Wagner's dun pony seemed to be running at an awkward gait.

There was a time to flee and a time to hold up to take a measure of the enemy. Trace pulled up the gray as they reached a clump of live-oaks to assess their chances. He saw no one pursuing on horseback, and so for a moment there was time to catch their breath and regroup.

'Keep running, you fool!' Ben Torrance said as he sat his lathered dun.

'Let's see who's coming – if anyone,' Trace said to the nervous man.

Curt had drawn up now too, and he said, 'They got my horse in the flank. I'll have to walk him.'

Johnny Johnson, in high spirits, sat his paint pony reloading his pistol. 'I guess we showed them something,' he said confidently. 'I think I got at least one of them.'

'Trace!' Ben Torrance said wildly, his face flushed in the moonlight, 'they'll be coming soon.'

'Settle down,' Curt Wagner said. 'It'll take them awhile to gather their horses and equip them. I think we're better off leading them away from the camp for a way, what do you say, Trace?'

'That's a thought – so long as we don't take too much time about it. We'll circle back to camp. Once we're in the Tanglewood no one's going to track us down anyway. At least not in silence. I think we should split up. There's enough moon left for them to follow our tracks yet, but they'll have to split their force and decide which of four trails they wish to pursue.

'I think Curt should ride straight toward the Tanglewood – his horse has a nasty limp. The rest of us will lead them on a merry chase for a while.'

'I don't see what's so merry about it,' Ben Torrance grumbled. 'I can't ride far or fast carrying this sack of gold.'

'Do your best, Ben. At least set a false trail for half an hour or so. Now, let's start before they have caught up their ponies and saddled them.'

'I want to go too,' the strange yet familiar, high-pitched voice said, and the woman rode out of the oaks to join them in the moonlight. 'I have to get to Danny,' Kate Cousins said.

'Danny?' Curt Wagner said blankly before he understood that she meant Dan Sumner.

'I know he's in the Tanglewood – he told me so. But I've been searching and I can't find a trail into it.'

The woman was no more than twenty with dark hair and brown eyes. Her face was still girlish, not formed into womanhood. Nor was her body. Her mouth was set with determination.

'Hell,' Ben Torrance complained, 'that's not possible.'

'Dan's been shot, Kate,' Trace Dawson told her.

'I know that. I was there when it happened,' the young woman replied. 'Why do you think I need to find him? I have to help him!'

'I don't know what you can do,' Trace said.

'Just take me to him,' she said, looking from Trace to Curt Wagner, then to Johnny Johnson.

'Trace?' Curt Wagner asked. There wasn't time to sit debating the matter. Trace nodded his agreement.

'Ride ahead with Curt,' Trace said, giving his consent. To the others he said, 'The three of us had better make tracks.'

Trace watched silently as the tall man on the injured dun rode ahead with the frantic young woman. He sighed, kicked his unfortunate gray horse on the flank, and began a twisting and puzzling ride which would lead eventually back into the depths of the Tanglewood.

Johnny Johnson, Trace noticed, had lingered a little longer than the others, following the receding form of Kate Cousins into the night shadows with his eyes. Trace hoped that there was nothing to that. They did not need any sort of trouble between their two young riders now that the war had begun; he knew such situations could be combustible where young blood was concerned.

'Hit the spurs, Johnny,' he called back after a minute when the kid had still not started his paint pony on to the night trail.

Trace rode silently, weaving his way on a devious course. He frequently looked back toward the town and the road to the Tanglewood, but he saw no pursuing riders. Maybe Prince Blakely and Storm Ross could not

21

be found or, if they were awakened, had considered pursuit a futile endeavor in the night. Maybe not enough sober, willing men could be found to form a posse. At any rate, they seemed to have eluded the townsmen.

For now.

The Blakely-Ross men would be doubly alert from here on, and they would make their try eventually. When they did it would make tonight's brief battle look like child's play.

Dan Sumner lifted his eyes then sprang to his feet as rapidly as his gunshot-leg would allow. He drew his Colt revolver, positioned himself behind the shelter of a sagging sycamore limb and steeled his nerves. A voice called out softly:

'It's Curt, Dan.'

Was he the only one who had made it back?

Dan limped forward, still not holstering his handgun. The moonlight slanted on him from the west as it faded toward the distant Rocky Mountains. Dan Sumner had a hundred questions running through his mind, but he forgot them all immediately.

It could not be, but it was. Kate Cousins sat her little pony beside the tall, broad-shouldered Curt Wagner. Curt helped her down from her saddle, and before her boots had hit the ground, Dan was to her, taking her into his arms.

There was a lot of cooing and murmuring as Curt Wagner considerately turned away and began unsaddling his wounded horse. In fact Curt, rugged trailsman that he was, was embarrassed by such displays of affection.

Eventually Dan, his arm still loosely draped over Kate's shoulder asked Wagner, 'How did it go, Curt? Where are the others?'

'All things considered, it went very well,' Curt answered, placing his saddle aside. 'The others are circling the camp to try to throw off any trackers. The only casualty was Peso,' he said, stroking his horse's neck. 'I can't do much about that in this light.' The dun had a pained look in its eye, but besides cocking its right hind leg up to relieve it of its weight, the dun did not seem badly hurt.

'Here comes someone,' Kate Cousins said, and both men stiffened, reaching toward their guns, but a voice called out, 'It's Johnny!'

As they watched, Johnny Johnson and his paint pony separated themselves from the tangle of shadows and entered the camp.

'No pursuit?' Curt asked as the young man swung down.

'None that I saw.' Johnny added, 'It seems that Trace was being a little too cautious, sending us riding in all directions.'

'You can't be too cautious,' Curt replied.

'I see you made it,' Johnny said, eyeing Kate in a way that Dan Sumner found he did not care for.

'Of course I made it,' she answered. She looped an arm around Dan's waist. 'I need to be with my man.'

She said it in a way that was meant to squelch any romantic ideas Johnny Johnson might have been harboring. Kate was still young but she had worked as a barmaid in her father's saloon for three years and had learned early on how to fend off unwanted advances from men.

'I got at least two of them,' Johnny Johnson bragged to Dan Sumner. Curt Wagner cocked his head but said nothing – the story was bound to get bigger in the telling. Dan Sumner was unimpressed and concentrating his thoughts elsewhere.

'Good for you,' Dan replied. Then he turned Kate away from the other two men and let her help him as he limped back toward the sycamore where he had spread his ground-sheet. Johnny watched them with obvious envy in his eyes.

Curt Wagner who had been following all of the byplay without seeming to, said in a low voice, 'Don't play with fire, son.'

Johnson snapped, 'He doesn't even know what fire is yet!' He might have gone on, but at that moment they heard another horse arriving and turned to see Trace walking his big gray into the camp.'

'Where's Torrance?' Curt inquired.

'Probably got himself lost,' Johnny Johnson said as he stamped away toward his own bedroll.

'What's the matter with the kid?' Trace asked as he swung down, tossing the heavy sack of gold he had been carrying to Curt.

'I'll tell you later,' Curt replied. 'There's a small problem and you're the only one who can handle it.'

'Oh?' Trace Dawson said, his forehead corrugating as he frowned. Then he glanced toward the sycamore where young Kate Cousins sat, cheek to cheek with Dan Sumner and he nodded his understanding. 'I'll take care of it in the morning, Curt. If I can't, someone will have to go.'

At last just before midnight, Ben Torrance trailed in, his pale face looked exhausted, and as sadly pessimistic as ever. He had tied the burlap sack he had been carrying since the bank robbery to his pommel. The knots had tightened with hard riding and his fingers fumbled with the knots. Curt stepped to Ben's horse and untied the knots as the man swung heavily down.

'Well, that was quite a night!' Ben Torrance said with forced joviality. 'Are we all back safe and sound?'

'For tonight,' Trace said. He was worried about the durability of the heavy man, about his ability and willingness to follow through with their plan. Ben Torrance seemed done in already. Perhaps when morning came he would find himself with more than one problem to deal with. For now, after a quick glance at the young lovers sleeping closely together, at a fidgety Johnny Johnson and at Ben Torrance who had ridden in so exhausted that he hadn't bothered to remove his boots and hat before falling into his blankets, there was nothing for Trace to do but curl up in his own bed, let the fading moon run over and try to find the comfort of sleep in the uneasy silence of the Tanglewood. With the settling of the moon beyond the mountain peaks, only its lingering aura left behind to remind them of its passing, the clouds crowded the sky and the seemingly sentient night closed its starry eyes.

No one even heard the newcomer approach the

camp, unsaddle his horse and sit cross-legged near the cold fire to outwait the dawn.

'Well!' Prince Blakely said unhappily. He paced his own library with its highly polished oak floor, a snifter of brandy in hand. His long-time partner, Storm Ross, watching the blond man with the thinning hair and hint of a paunch, decided that Prince was half-drunk and probably had the right to be. The town bank had been robbed, Storm Ross, the banker, knew it was potentially ruinous. Storm said nothing immediately. Small, lean, sober, Storm Ross was given to thought in advance of action. Prince Blakely was a bull-headed, charge-at-them type of man. They made ideal business partners.

'What does Kaylin Standish say?' Storm asked after a minute of staring at the fire curlicueing in the white stone hearth.

'Standish!' Prince Blakely said in frustration, finishing his drink and pouring himself another from a cut-glass decanter. 'Why did we ever bring him in? He's afraid to go into the Tanglewood, that's obvious.'

'That wasn't what we brought him in for,' Storm Ross said reasonably. 'He'd had experience as a town marshal and proven himself to be . . . flexible in matters of law enforcement. Unlike Trace Dawson.'

'I know, I know,' Blakely said, standing close to the hearth where a log burned behind the brass andirons and blue smoke curled away from the chimney into the night skies. 'But something has to be done. All of our capital is gone, all of our legal records. I was over at the bank tonight – they didn't miss a trick, whoever it was.'

'It has to be Trace Dawson who's behind it, and maybe Dan Sumner. He was seen earlier, eyeing the situation here. Kaylin Standish shot him.'

'I know all of that,' Blakely said miserably, running a harried hand across his thinning scalp. 'I can guess who the others were, but what now, Ross?'

'Did Standish flatly refuse to go into the Tanglewood?'

'Well, not exactly,' Blakely demurred, his anger seeming to abate. 'He just told me that in his opinion it was impossible to enter silently, to track down anyone there who wanted to remain hidden without the certainty of being sniped at. I'll ask him again in the morning.'

'He's right,' Storm Ross said. 'It would probably be suicidal for one man – or twenty. But' – Ross went on, rising from his leather chair, adjusting the creases in his trousers – 'I wouldn't worry about it, Prince. Help is already on the way. I've seen to it. We are equal partners, after all. Maybe we should have anticipated this, but we didn't. Now all we can do is make sure it doesn't have a lasting impact or happen again.'

'Help?' Prince Blakely said blankly. 'But who. . . ?'

'The Clinch Mountain gang,' Storm said, taking his silver-gray hat from the round table beside his chair, placing it on his head. 'It will cost a few dollars, but they are capable of taking care of the problem. Being outlaws themselves, they are well versed in the ways of thieves.'

Who in hell. . . ? Trace Dawson opened one eye to the

27

morning light then closed it quickly. When he opened it again it was with utmost caution, only a slit between his eyelids showing. His right hand had slithered down toward his holster like a creeping insect.

Dawn was bright and reddish-gold through the branches of the oaks. The river could be heard babbling beyond the underbrush. The camp was still asleep except for the stranger who was calmly sitting, going through the contents of the burlap bags containing the stolen bank money and court papers.

The man, Trace saw, was of average build, clean-shaven, well put together. His fawn-colored Stetson hat was tilted back from his forehead. Trace rose with his gun in his hand.

'Before I shoot you, just who are you and what in hell do you think you're doing!'

CHAPTER THREE

Laredo placed down the documents he had been studying and shifted his eyes to the man challenging him. Carefully he put the papers back in one of the burlap bags; carefully he rose, keeping his hand away from the stag-handled Colt revolver he wore on his hip. To his left he now saw another man rise from his bed, wearing a hatchet on his belt – a necessary implement in the Tanglewood, and still another man with a Winchester in his hands, blinking at him through the morning sunlight.

'My name is Laredo. I was sent up here to do a job,' he explained. At their uncomprehending looks, he went on, 'I am with the enforcement arm of the Arizona Bank Examiners' office.'

'The Arizona Territory's line is about twenty miles south,' said one of the late risers, Johnny Johnson.

'Yes, it is,' Laredo said placatingly. 'But Colorado does not have a system like ours in place. There were a lot of complaints about the Lordsberg bank that they weren't able to investigate out of Denver; they requested our assistance.'

'It only happened last night!' Johnny Johnson, the

29

man Laredo had noticed holding a hatchet, shouted frantically.

Laredo did not respond to him, but kept his eyes fixed on Trace Dawson who seemed to be the leader and the most dangerous among them. It was obvious to Laredo that these men had done something larcenous overnight – bank robbery. There were bundles of fresh, uncirculated bank notes in the burlap bags, and a quantity of gold coins. That would all have to be straightened out by the Colorado authorities. It was not his job to do so. He had not the license to arrest or prosecute, but simply to investigate.

'Boys,' Laredo said, rising lazily, his eyes still on Trace Dawson's Colt revolver and Johnson's hatchet, 'I was sent here to look into a number of shady enterprises that the Lordsberg bank was involved in. Heavy-handed land-grabs, illegal evictions, confiscation of private property. You'd be better served by letting me work with you than against you.' He nodded toward the burlap sacks at his feet. 'Otherwise you're just digging yourselves a deeper grave.'

'What are you proposing?' Trace Dawson asked the man called Laredo.

'I have a lot of people working with me in Tucson who are quite competent where legal matters are involved,' Laredo responded. 'I'd like to take the disputed deeds down there with me and have them look them over.'

'Take our deeds!' Johnny Johnson said angrily. The young man still held his hatchet beside his leg.

'Technically,' Laredo answered, 'they're not yours at

all. They're stolen property from the bank of Lordsberg.'

'I suppose you want to take the gold and currency as well,' Ben Torrance said, his habitually sad face now tight with anger.

'I would if I thought I could carry it all,' Laredo said with a grin. 'And if I thought it would resolve matters. But I can't and it wouldn't. I don't think I can arrest you four without a lot of trouble, so let me see what I can do working with you. I don't think you are thieves, just men driven to desperate measures.'

'*Technically*,' Johnny Johnson said with some belliger-ence as he repeated the word Laredo had used, 'you don't have any right to do anything at all. You're not in Arizona now, are you?'

'No, I'm not,' Laredo said evenly. 'If you think there is someone else handy to help you out of your predica-ment, tell me. Go to him. Although by now I imagine there's a price on all of your heads and if you leave the Tanglewood, you're in serious danger of being arrested – or worse,' he said turning his cold eyes now on the very young-appearing Kate Cousins who had come forward to cling to Dan Sumner's arm.

'He's right, I'm afraid,' Trace Dawson said with some weariness. By an unvoiced vote he had assumed the role of leader of the gang. As a former cavalry officer, he was simply more experienced than the others, but this was beyond his experience. Robbing the Lordsberg bank had seemed like a fine idea, but now Trace could see that it was leading them no closer to a solution to their problems. 'Let Laredo have the legal documents – maybe something can be done,' he muttered, his voice falling to a near whisper.

'They're all we have,' Ben Torrance complained.

'None of them is of any value to us. They're all in Blakely's or Ross's name.'

'We could—' Curt Wagner began, but it was going to be a futile suggestion. What could they do? Petition the court in Lordsberg? 'Ah, hell, Laredo, take them and see if there's anything to be done.'

Laredo placed the handful of documents in his saddle-bags, swung aboard his thick-chested buckskin horse, touched his hatbrim in farewell, and turned away silently in the Tanglewood.

'I don't like this,' Johnny Johnson said bitterly. 'We don't even know who the man is.'

'Forget it, Johnny,' Dan Sumner said, placing a friendly arm across Johnny's shoulder. 'The legal papers weren't doing us any good anyway.'

'The idea was to get Prince Blakely and Storm Ross honking mad,' Curt Wagner said. 'And you can bet they are by now.'

'The bank won't be doing much business today, that's for sure,' Trace Dawson said. He crouched down and tipped his hat back. 'I guess the question is – what do we do next?'

'I've been thinking about that,' Johnson said with a sly grin. 'We could ruin their water supply. Find some arsenic and put it in Ben Torrance's well.'

'Poison my well!' the bald man was aghast.

'It *was* yours,' Johnny said with a dirty little smirk.

'That's flat-out murder,' Kate Cousins who had been holding her tongue, said.

'I don't like that idea,' Curt Wagner added, and the tall man crouched beside Trace Dawson, sketching figures in the dry earth with a twig.

'Nor do I,' Trace agreed. 'We'll say that one is voted off the table.'

'It would work!' Johnny protested loudly, but the others ignored him. He stepped away from Dan Sumner's friendly arm, but kept his more-than-friendly eyes on Kate Cousins who was well-aware of the kid's gaze. She had seen the same kind of look a hundred times in the Wabash Saloon.

'I'd like to know what Blakely and Ross figure on doing about this,' Dan Sumner said. 'And I think we ought to move our camp. If this Laredo found us, so can someone else.'

'You mean go deeper into the Tanglewood?' Ben Torrance said with apparent alarm. 'Some of it is almost impenetrable!'

'That's why I think it's a good idea,' Dan replied. He glanced at Kate who was already trembling. Perhaps she had over-estimated her nerve. He bent his head and whispered. 'You don't have to be here, Kate.'

'I know where I have to be!' she said so strongly that everyone heard her.

'Want me to ride into town and find a preacher to bring out here?' Johnny Johnson asked in a near sneer, watching the two of them.

'We'll find our own when the time is right,' Dan Sumner said coldly and Johnny slunk away, having received notice.

'He might be the one who has to go,' Curt Wagner

whispered to Trace as the young man moved away into the concealment of the blackthorn brush.

'I know,' Trace said heavily, rising to his feet. 'If it works out that way – well, I think we should not move our camp until after he's gone.'

'You think he'd turn traitor?'

'I don't know. I just— I'll try having a talk with him.'

'All right,' Curt said, stretching his long arms. 'You know, Trace, we still haven't decided on a plan, and I think it's important to keep the pressure on Blakely and Ross if we're to have any hope of winning.'

'I haven't forgotten,' Trace said as the two young lovers wandered off and Ben Torrance began morosely searching their stores looking for something to eat. 'I think I'm going to go into town to see how things stand.'

'You can't possibly!'

'I think I can. What if they're mounting a posse of twenty men or more and they storm upon us? We have to know.'

'Where would you—'

'To the Wabash. Word will already have spread to the saloons if they're mounting a posse.'

'You think that Gentry Cousins would let you shelter up there?' Curt asked in puzzlement.

'No. But I think Ruby would,' Trace answered.

'Oh,' Curt said carefully. 'I see.'

'I doubt that you do, but there's an outside staircase to her room. And she'll let me in.'

For a moment Trace studied Curt Wagner's face which had become unreadable. 'It will be all right, Curt,' Trace assured him. 'And I can at least get word to

34

Gentry Cousins that his daughter is safe.'

The two men walked to where they had left their horses, and once in the shelter of the scrub oaks, Trace asked, 'Where did you ever learn how to open a safe, Curt?'

Wagner laughed. 'Along my backtrail,' he said. 'You people elected me marshal, remember, and I was grateful for the job. I didn't feel that you needed to know everything about my background.' He clapped a hand on his friend's shoulder. 'I'll tell you all about it one day.'

Johnny Johnson sat brooding in the shelter of a tiny bower surrounded by sour oaks and blackthorn. For a while he had followed Kate and Dan Sumner furtively, like a shadow on their trail, but their whispered conversation, the occasional hugs and tender kisses had made his stomach turn with jealousy. What did Dan have that he did not?

Well, Kate Cousins for one thing.

He'd bet that if he was fixed up better he could have her. Hell, he could have other girls just as good, better than Kate.

Johnny lifted his eyes as Trace Dawson walked his gray horse away from the camp. Where was he going? It seemed that the older men, Trace and Curt Wagner, were reluctant to let him in on any of their plans. Old, bald Ben Torrance knew little more than Johnny did, but that was different. Ben was going to fat, cowardly, whereas Johnny was ready to go, to enter the fray with Prince Blakely and Storm Ross, but nothing was being done.

Maybe it was time to pull up stakes and head south

into Arizona. But what would he have there? Without money – but there was money. A lot of it.

Johnny sat in the copse, breaking small twigs into smaller pieces as he thought. *To hell with the Tanglewood.* He slapped at a swarm of gnats that had decided to gather around his head. *To hell, with Dan Sumner and Kate Cousins*! His own horse farm and cabin along the Wakapee had been stripped from him, but who was to say he couldn't start anew? If he only had some money – and didn't he deserve a cut of the proceeds from the Lordsberg bank job?

Trace and Curt Wagner hadn't even brought up the subject of splitting the loot. Perhaps because they had no intention of doing so. Maybe that was why they were so silent about their intentions – they meant to keep it all for themselves. Dan Sumner was too hypnotized by Kate Cousins's skirt to know what was going on around him. Ben Torrance was too old and cowardly to object. Besides, Ben had lost nothing but a water-well in the takeover of the Blakely-Ross group. He could always go out on to the desert and dig himself another hole in the ground.

Johnny rose, dusting his hands on his jeans. Then he started back toward camp. He meant to keep a close eye on the stolen money and, if the opportunity presented itself, to make his own cut of the loot. He knew of a good little section of land down Flagstaff way.

Ruby Rose Lee, or so she had named herself since coming West, slept late if not well in her room over the Wabash Saloon. Morning was the only hope of getting any sleep. Until well past midnight the saloon was filled with the roaring, rambunctious, raucous uncouth men drinking away whatever money they had in their jeans. And it was Ruby's job to stand around, smile, be man-handled and watch as they grew progressively drunker and more belligerent. It was the smiling that wore thin as the night rolled by and she was mauled, propositioned and fondled. That was all supposed to keep her smiling cheerfully, she supposed. As if that sort of activity could make any woman feel comfortable and friendly.

There was no end to the innuendo as she brought trays of drinks to their tables.

The cocky bastards.

Most of them stank. It was a rare thing to find a man who had bathed in recent memory, liquor being more important than a bathhouse. Those who did have a recent shave and tub-soak considered themselves to be irresistible after a splash of bay rum.

Ah, it was a hell of a way to make a living, Ruby thought as she lay half-awake in her sunlit room.

In her year in Lordsberg she had only met one man who even approached her expectation of what a man should be, and he. . . .

There was a tap on the pane of her half-glassed outer door, the one leading to the balcony and down a flight of steps to the alley below. She frowned and turned over in bed, not wishing to answer it, but the knocking was persistent and finally she rose, slipped into her candy-pink silk wrapper and walked suspiciously to the door. Peering out, she straightened up in surprise and reached immediately to unlock the door. The man with coppery hair and wide shoulders entered quickly, smelling of sagebrush and long travel.

'Trace!'

'It's me, Ruby.' He did not offer his arms, but she embraced the former town marshal uninvited.

'I thought you'd have fled to the far country,' Ruby said, taking his hand to guide him into the room after closing the shade.

'There was the temptation,' Trace admitted, sagging on to the familiar bed, tossing his hat on to the brass bedpost.

Ruby sat beside him, sweeping her wrapper and nightgown between her knees with both hands. 'Life's gone to hell around here with you gone,' she said with a small, practiced flutter of her eyelashes. She forced herself out of the expression. The coquettish look made her a lot of money with the drinking men, but this was Trace Dawson.

She went on, 'Kaylin Standish! They call him a lawman!' Her hand rested on Trace's briefly. 'Now Kate Cousins is missing.'

'I know,' Trace replied. 'That's one reason I came into town. I wanted to tell Gentry that his daughter's alright. We have her with us in the Tanglewood.'

'With Dan Sumner – well, I suppose she's safe enough,' Ruby said dubiously. Her lower lip was thrust out a fraction of an inch.

'She is,' Trace answered. 'You know the girl didn't belong in a place like this. If you'll get word to Gentry Cousins—'

'Gentry doesn't own the saloon anymore,' Ruby told him. Trace Dawson's eyebrows drew together in disbelief.

'I mean,' Ruby said, spreading her hands, 'he doesn't on the books. He was served notice that the Wabash Saloon was constructed illegally on land belonging to the township of Lordsberg.'

Trace rose to his feet and replied angrily, 'How can they say that! There was no township of Lordsberg when Gentry built the Wabash. Only empty land and a fur-trading post.'

Ruby shrugged. 'That's what they told him. They had some sort of legal papers to justify eviction.'

'Who,' Trace asked slowly, 'now owns the Wabash?'

'How many guesses would you need?' Ruby asked with a fleeting smile.

'Well,' Trace said, wondering if they had also taken the papers signed by Blakely and Ross's hired judge during the bank hold-up. 'Maybe their case isn't as strong as they believe.'

'They've got the law on their side,' Ruby said.

'For now.' He asked, 'Where's Gentry Cousins now?'

'I couldn't tell you. The last time I saw him he was drunker than any of his customers, threatening to kill Marshal Standish, Ross, Blakely and Judge Weems.'

'That's not the way to go about it,' Trace Dawson said. Ruby's small hand had returned to rest on his. Near to her now he could almost taste the faint woman-scent of her.

'What is the right way to go about it?' Ruby asked. Her eyelashes did not flutter; her dark eyes remained fixed on Trace's.

'I don't know. I wish I did. We're kind of trying to figure that out – me and Curt Wagner and Dan Sumner.'

'And Johnson and Ben Torrance?'

Trace's eyes narrowed. 'How did you know about them?'

Ruby laughed, but not with amusement. 'It's kind of hard not to figure it out when they've got reward notices on all of you posted around town.'

'Have they?' Trace asked, putting his other hand over Ruby's.

She nodded, turned her eyes down again and asked, 'Did you have anything to do with the bank robbery, Trace?'

'Me! Of course not,' he said, his falsehood so transparent that it was not intended to be believed.

'It's very dangerous for you here. Why did you ride into town, Trace?' Ruby asked with concern.

'Well, I wanted to see Gentry Cousins or at least get word to him that his daughter was alright. Secondly, more importantly, I guess, was I wanted to see how much of an uproar we had caused and try to figure a way to hit Blakely and Ross again so that next time, if anything, it would hurt them even more.'

'Anything else?' Ruby asked.

'I don't know,' he said. 'You know I was wondering if we'd done right by young Dan Sumner. I was watching him and Kate Cousins together. Just a couple of kids with miles and miles to go in their lives.'

Ruby lifted her dark eyes again to Trace. Her lips were parted slightly, hesitant, before she smiled at him. 'I've got a few miles left in me, Trace.'

'I know you do, Ruby. That's the other reason I rode in here.'

CHAPTER FOUR

Curt Wagner felt weighted down by a settling uneasiness. All morning he had had the uncomfortable feeling that something was wrong. Since Trace had ridden off toward Lordsberg the feeling of menace had grown. And why had Trace made that dangerous ride? Only to see Ruby? If so he was acting the same way, making the same mistakes, as the kids were.

Curt, too, loved the women but there was a time and a place for them. The Tanglewood was not the place, and this certainly wasn't the time. He kept a curry comb in his saddle-bags and he walked to his dun horse now to smooth the faithful animal's coat.

'I don't like the way this is shaping up,' he said and the dun horse's ear twitched toward him. There were suddenly too many uncertainties: for example, should they expel Johnny Johnson from the gang or not? Was Dan Sumner to be relied upon now that he was caught up in some youthful romantic fantasy? Trace was – well, Trace was their leader but what was his plan? Ben Torrance only sulked now, looking as if he regretted ever having joined the gang.

Curt continued to brush his horse wondering about the fix they were in. They were now burdened with gold they had sworn not to spend but which they could not return. The bank job had seemed a grand idea at the time, but what had it actually accomplished? They had to worry about toting the gold, currency and court papers around with them unless they left them in some pit to molder. It seemed they had made only a futile gesture of defiance.

And what about this man called Laredo? Curt asked himself. Who was he, really, and why had they trusted him? He had shown them no badge, no warrants, no proof of his identity, but now he held the deeds not only to Trace Dawson's cattle ranch, but to Johnny Johnson's small spread and Ben Torrance's water rights. Dan Sumner's place as well. Hell, half of the outlying Wakapee Valley! They might as well have let Blakely and Ross have their way, Curt thought angrily. All they had achieved was outlawing themselves.

'Oh, well,' Curt said softly to the horse, 'I suppose it's what we bargained for.'

'Just when do you intend to do something about it, Standish!' Prince Blakely demanded angrily. The stout little man paced the floor of the marshal's office like a marching general. His aide-de-camp, Storm Ross, was not there in the sun-heated room. Ross was still at the bank, estimating their losses.

Kaylin Standish, who was not a quick-moving man, stretched his legs and rubbed his lantern jaw. 'I'm still trying to come up with a plan, Mister Blakely. It's no easy task going into the Tanglewood.'

'Burn them out! Burn the whole Tanglewood. What use is it to man or nature anyway?'

'That's a thought,' the dark-eyed marshal said without rising from his chair, 'but if the fire got out of hand it might shift toward the prairie and the wind would drive it straight on to Lordsberg. I don't think that's a workable plan.'

'You're afraid to go in there, is that it?' Blakely asked, wiping a hand across his thinning blond hair.

'I don't know if that's the right word, Mr. Blakely. Afraid? Not really,' Standish said shaking his head. 'But there's roughly a thousand square miles of the Tanglewood, and there's places a horse can't penetrate. Places where nothing larger than a rattler can slither through. We don't know where they've got their camp. We could spend days, weeks, even months looking for it.

'The best thing to do is wait until they come out – they'll have to eventually.'

'By then we'll be ruined,' Blakely said, leaning his fists on the marshal's desk. 'With the bank now raided.'

'You'll make it fine, Mr. Blakely,' the marshal said lazily. 'You always have.'

'I suppose we will,' Blakely replied, his face turning stony. 'How will *you* make it when we no longer have the funds to pay your salary? Listen to me – I want those men and I want what they looted from the bank. And I want it now!'

It was not only the stolen money, Blakely was thinking as he stepped out of the marshal's office into the cold sunlight, but the loss of all of their legal papers – deeds to the outlying property, promissory notes, land titles, everything he and Ross had worked so hard to accumulate to build their own empire on the Western range. True, he could dig into his personal money kept in a safe at home and pay functionaries like the marshal and Judge Weems. But of what use were those two under the present circumstances?

Damn the Tanglewood gang! They had to be captured or killed. Obviously Kaylin Standish wasn't the man for the job. They needed some outside help. Men without fear. And for that kind of help Blakely would raid his own hidden cash. But he knew of no such men.

Ross had said that he had a way of calling in the notorious Clinch Mountain boys. Was that the truth or a boast? It was time to put it to the test.

It was time.

When the wind blew, she trembled. It was growing late in the year and the chilling wind funneled down off the slopes of the Rocky Mountains. Sitting beside Dan Sumner, Kate Cousins drew her knees up, looped her arms around them and shivered. It had seemed a romantic, bold adventure to pursue the man she loved into the Tanglewood, but she had never imagined a place like this. All snarls and thorns and small, slithering, venomous things. She thought, 'Misery is the essence of this place.'

The sun had briefly shone, but somehow its rays never seemed to strike the earth through the jumble of tangled, misshapen trees. It was hardly her imagined Sherwood Forest. The bogs stank, and large animals that seemed to have no fear of man prowled nearby. Insects continued their infuriating, relentless assault on any uncovered bit of flesh. The place was simply horrid. She had to find a way to coax Dan into leaving the wilds. Where they would go, she had no idea; perhaps her father would be willing to help them. But how. . . ?

'I think it's festering,' Dan Sumner said, grimacing as he clutched his wounded leg above the knee where Marshal Standish's bullet had struck him.

'Let me see,' Kate Cousins said, scooting toward him, her eyes dark with concern. 'Drop your trousers.'

'I can't do that,' Dan said stubbornly although pain was marking his face.

'Oh, for heaven's sake!' Kate said. 'Let me have a look at it. I've seen wounds before.'

'But not—'

'I've seen a man's leg before too, believe it or not,' Kate said with irritation, managing to put some kindness in the tone of her scolding. 'Now, young man' she instructed him firmly, 'drop your trousers.'

Dan Sumner, it seemed, was much more embarrassed than Kate at having her examine him, but he complied. There was too much pain to be ignored. Perhaps something could be done. Kate ran her fingers gently over the swollen area of his leg where an infection had set in around the bullet hole Kaylin Standish had drilled there. Kate sat back on her knees.

'Do you men have anything like carbolic in camp?'

'No,' Dan answered. 'We left town with little more

than our ponies and our guns.'

Kate shook her head, still studying the red, suppurating wound. 'We've got to get you some help, Dan. You're right about that. Otherwise. . . .'

Dan was tugging his trousers back up awkwardly. He knew what she was trying to say. Otherwise he might lose that leg if not his life. He looked at her pinched mouth and concerned eyes and tried to smile for her.

'All right then, we'll get some help. Where?'

'Lordsberg, of course. There's no other place for fifty miles, no place with a doctor for a hundred.'

'But I—' Dan started to object.

'You had no part in the bank robbery, did you!'

'Only because I got myself wounded.'

'They can't hang a man for what he might have considered doing, Dan!'

'They can – in Lordsberg,' he answered quietly.

'Your life, our life, is at stake here, Dan. I won't let our future be taken from us. Can you ride that far?'

'I guess I'll have to,' Dan Sumner said, giving into the inevitable. It was either a long, lingering death from inaction or a quick snap of his neck at the end of the rope. Kate helped him to his feet and he hobbled back to the camp, leaning heavily on her. Dan paused to have a short talk with Curt Wagner as Kate went to retrieve their ponies.

'Well, I don't see what else you can do,' the tall man replied with a frown when Dan had finished explaining.

'Don't worry about me giving up the location of the camp, Curt.'

'That's the last thing I'd worry about, Dan.' He put a

hand briefly on Sumner's shoulder. 'Just watch yourself. If you're careful, you might be able to slip into town without being caught.'

'I think we're going to Kate's father's house and send for a doctor.'

'That might be the best plan,' Curt said as Kate arrived with their horses. Her young face was grim; her eyes older than her years. Curt gave Dan a lift up into the saddle, and felt a strange sort of envy as he watched the two young people weave their way along the secret Tanglewood trail. They did have a lot of miles to go, but they had each other to travel with. Shaking off his pensive mood, Curt Wagner started thinking now about where that left him. He had only himself, Johnny Johnson and Ben Torrance – who seemed ready to give up the whole business.

Where was Trace!

Trace had made a scouting expedition into Lordsberg, but he was hours overdue. If he had learned anything new, he should have been eager to get back and tell them about it. Curt had a sudden unkind image of Trace lying up in bed with Ruby, forgetting about his trail mate. But that was not Trace Dawson. He had gotten into some sort of a jam.

And there was no way Curt could go looking for him, leaving Johnny and Ben Torrance alone with the proceeds of the bank stick-up.

Their plan was falling apart rapidly.

It was by the dawn light that the door to Ruby's room was kicked in and Trace Dawson had no chance of grabbing his Colt, hung in its belt-holster around the post of the brass bed. He simply sat up and lifted his hands above his head. Ruby stood to one side, drawing her candy-pink wrapper more tightly around her as if it were a protective cocoon.

'I told you I saw him, Marshal,' said one of the men, a whiskered rummy, eager to take credit for the capture – and possibly for the reward if one had been posted.

'Yeah, you did,' Kaylin Standish said, his gun trained on Trace. 'Now get out of here and give us some room to work.'

Beside Standish stood two other men, both burly, both armed with Colt revolvers. Trace did not recognize either of them. Standish let his eyes linger on Ruby, standing in front of the silhouetting sunlit window.

'Can't keep a bee away from its honey,' Standish said. 'You and that Dan Sumner alike. Both of you fools for that honey.'

'Shut up,' Trace growled.

'Get your pants on!' Kaylin Standish ordered sharply. 'I'm going to lock you up where you won't be getting any honey for a long time.'

'They'll break me out,' Trace told Standish, who looked only briefly worried.

'How many men have you got riding with you Trace?' he asked slyly.

'Twenty, maybe thirty. We've got the gold to pay them now.'

Standish laughed. 'You're a liar,' the marshal said. But a vague uncertainty lingered in his eyes as Trace finished dressing and stamping into his boots.

'Let's get going,' Standish said. 'Grab your hat, Trace, though I don't think you'll have much use for it for a while. Marvin, bring his belt gun along,' he nodded toward the pistol still hanging in its holster on the brass headboard. Trace shrugged and started toward the hall door.

'Not that way!' Standish said. 'The way you came in: the back entrance. There's men in the saloon downstairs. They're about evenly divided between those who think you're some kind of hero and those who would like to lynch you on sight. Let's do this with as little trouble as possible.'

Ruby's fingertips went to her lips as she watched them push Trace out the back entrance and descend the wooden steps toward the alleyway below. She listened to their clomping boots until the morning went silent again; then she sat on her bed and lowered her face to her hands.

When Dan Sumner reached the town limits of Lordsberg, he and Kate decided to avoid the main street and travel by the back alleys towards Gentry Cousins's house on the outskirts. To ride through the center of town in broad daylight was too hazardous by far. No sooner had they entered one of dark, narrow byways than Dan reined in his horse, squinted into the morning sun and told Kate:

'Run for it. Get out of the way. There might be shooting.'

Kate hesitated briefly, and then saw what Dan had seen. Kaylin Standish and two of his deputies escorting

Trace Dawson along the alley directly toward them.

'Dan—' she said, but she could see that her man had made his mind up. She turned her horse to one side, taking a secondary alleyway toward the cottonwood grove north of town.

Dan watched the four men approaching him, tugged his hat lower, took a deep breath, and walked his horse in their direction. In the meanwhile he had taken his boot from his left stirrup, leaving it to dangle empty. He was less than twenty feet from the approaching party when he nudged the horse with his boot heels, startling it into a run.

'Trace!' Dan called out and four heads came up to stare in his direction. He drove his horse between Trace and his guards, knocking Marshal Kaylin to the ground. Trace was able to thrust his boot toe into the empty stirrup, and by clinging to the saddle cantle, to hold on to the pony's side as Dan Sumner raced it toward the head of the alley.

Too surprised to fire their guns immediately, the guards only belatedly unholstered their weapons and let loose four poorly-aimed shots in their direction, but by then the horse had cleared the alley entrance and Dan had it running toward the cottonwood grove, Trace holding on for dear life.

Dan drew up his horse among the trees to let Trace reposition himself, but he waited for a minute, looking around the grove. He had hoped to find Kate waiting there for him, but she was not.

'We'd better get moving,' Trace said. 'They could be right behind us.'

'Not unless they're a lot quicker than they looked. See here, Trace, I'm not going back to the Tanglewood.'

'You're quitting?' Trace asked in disbelief.

'No, it's not that. It's my leg; it's in bad shape. I'm liable to lose it if I don't get some medical help.'

'I see. What did you have in mind, then?'

'I'm going to the Cousins's house. I'll have a doctor sent for.'

'Sounds risky.'

'It is, but what choice to I have? We can ride out to the house together and then you can take my pony back to the Tanglewood. I've got a feeling Curt might need you back there.'

'Johnny, you mean?'

'I don't know, but I could tell that Curt was worried when I left. He wants to move the camp, but not until the business with Johnny is straightened out – if it can be.'

'I don't like leaving you here alone,' Trace said.

'I have a better chance on my own, Trace. What can you do anyway?'

Trace thought it over. 'There are two doctors in town now, you know. Make sure you send for the new man, Campbell. Doctor Rivers is friendly with Blakely and Ross.'

'All right. I'll remember that. Now, we'd better get riding.'

It took them another half an hour to reach Gentry Cousins's house on the outskirts of town. Dan was relieved to see Kate's horse tied to the white-painted hitch rail in front. From the doorway a sullen Gentry Cousins, rifle in hands, watched their approach.

'The man is not happy with us,' Trace muttered.

'It's mostly me, I expect,' Dan answered. 'He thinks I lured his daughter into the wild country and got her involved in the doings of a band of desperadoes.'

'You can talk that out between you later. For now, we'd better get you into the house. I'll let your horse have some water and a little rest before I circle back the long way around to Tanglewood.'

Dan only nodded. His eyes were on the white curtains at the front windows of the house where he had seen a flutter of movement. Kate was watching for him; that was all that mattered at the moment.

Trace slipped down from the back of the horse and raised a friendly hand to Gentry Cousins. The gesture was not returned. The saloon-keeper's face was grim. No wonder – he had been thrown out of his place of business and now would probably lose his house, having no way to support it. He was plain mad, probably not specifically at Trace or Dan Sumner, but at the whole stinking little town of Lordsberg which had confiscated the property he had worked for years establishing.

Dan still sat his saddle. Now he said weakly, 'Trace, I'm going to need some help getting down.'

'Your leg that bad, is it?'

'It's getting that way.'

'All right, then,' Trace said. The former lawman supported Dan's weight while he swung down gingerly and limped uneasily toward the door.

'You're not coming into my home, Dan Sumner!'

Gentry Cousins said with heartfelt menace, levering a round into the chamber of his Winchester rifle.

'Oh, yes he is!' The front door had been flung open and Kate stood there, her hair disarranged, her eyes defiant. 'If you don't let him in, Father, then you can say goodbye – to both of us.'

CHAPTER FIVE

Dan Sumner lay in a sunny room on a comfortable bed. The doctor, Steven Campbell, a new arrival in Lordsberg who had no idea who Dan Sumner was, had come and gone, cleaning up the wound in his leg and bandaging it neatly.

After an hour to let the horse rest, Trace Dawson had departed for the Tanglewood to look into the situation there. No one had come looking for Dan. They had outdistanced the law, although there was always the threat that even the slow-witted Marshal Standish would put two and two together and guess that he had taken shelter in the Cousins's house.

Kate had sat in a chair nearby, watching as the doctor worked, watching as Dan slowly drifted off to sleep, but now when he opened his eyes, she was gone. A trace of her scent lingered there. Probably she had gone to bathe and change her trail-dusty clothes.

And to try to mollify her father whose understandable anger over the confiscation of his property had transferred itself to Dan Sumner with whom his only daughter had threatened to leave his home, and take up the outlaw trail! Gentry Cousins had not been seen while the doctor was here, and not since, but he was out there somewhere, perhaps letting his simmering anger focus on revenge. Against Prince Blakely and Storm Ross.

Or on Dan Sumner.

Dan yawned and sat up a little. He was not too uncomfortable so long as he avoided sudden movements. But how long would it take until he was fit to ride, to fight? He felt that he was letting the Tanglewood gang down, but he could not help it. For the moment he was warm, coddled, and at peace.

The door opened letting in a newly-bathed Kate Cousins, her hair brushed and pinned up, wearing a pretty yellow dress. She looked younger and older at once. Her eyes were bright as she crossed the room, kissed Dan's forehead once, and sat in the chair beside his bed once again, taking his hand tenderly.

'They're here, Kaylin,' said Standish's burly deputy, Jake Fromm, opening the door to the marshal's office.

'Good, then I can let you and Marvin go!' Kaylin Standish said, rising from his desk.

'Why us?' Jake, apparently stunned, asked.

'What did you two do to keep Trace Dawson from escaping?'

'Aw, Kaylin, what were we to do to help? Stand in the way of a running horse to slow it down?'

Kaylin Standish did not answer. He was irritated. Already Prince Blakely had hinted that he would be fired if he didn't do something to stop the Tanglewood mob. Well, he had captured their leader, Trace Dawson – and then let him escape.

Standish walked to his office door and peered out into the bright sunlight. Storm Ross, true to his word, had brought in a bunch of the Clinch Mountain boys. They were rough and ready men, no doubt about that. Which side of the law they were on was open to question. It depended, Kaylin supposed, on which paid the best. Right now it was Blakely and Ross who were putting up the cash.

The men were strung out along the street. A few had already wandered into the Wabash Saloon, leaving their sweating horses unattended at the hitch rails.

'How many of them are there?' Standish wanted to know.

'I counted seventeen. There might be a few more straggling in,' Jake replied. 'Think it's enough?'

'I don't know!' the marshal, still irritable, answered his disgraced deputy. Standish doubted that fifty men, a hundred, would be enough to sweep the desperadoes out of the Tanglewood, but the presence of the Clinch Mountain boys brought him a measure of comfort. The Tanglewood gang would think twice before making another incursion into Lordsberg.

Why they would even bother was the question. If Kaylin Standish had the money they had stolen from the bank, he would consider that he had made his point, and flee with his profits to new territory. But there was something different about those men. What it was, he could only guess. He put his hat on and went out into the cool sunlight to find the leader of the Clinch Mountain boys. Because something had to be done about the Tanglewood desperadoes.

Johnny Johnson watched as Curt Wagner walked away from the camp, rifle over his shoulder, held by the barrel, to scare up a deer for provisions. Dan Sumner and Trace Dawson were still gone on some errand or another. Ben Torrance spent most of his time sleeping or fretting. The old man even blubbered in his sleep, Johnny had heard him. Well, let him sit there cursing his fate; Johnny had had enough.

He meant to make his own fate.

To buy his way out of the Tanglewood and its misery. There were stacked thunderheads moving in from the north on the cold wind as Johnny Johnson went to saddle his paint pony. He passed the carelessly-strewn burlap bags containing the loot from the bank hold-up. There was enough in there for a new life, for sure. He would take only his share, and in currency. The gold would only slow him down, and he meant to be long gone from the Tanglewood before anyone even realized it.

The so-called gang was a joke. They were now reduced to only three men, and men with no apparent plan on how to proceed. Well, Johnny had a plan. He would hit Phoenix or Tucson, maybe even New Mexico, with his saddle-bags filled with money. Then he could do anything he wished. Start a new horse ranch, buy the affection of a dozen women, prettier and more accommodating than the haughty little Kate Cousins. He meant to travel the little-known south trail which wound along the river, even deeper into the Tanglewood but terminated, he believed, on the boundary of the open desert beyond.

The law in Lordsberg could not possibly know of the trail, and Johnny was certain that he could elude them. As to the Tanglewood gang, what there was of it, they would not be aware that he had taken anything until he had a lead of many miles on them. If they tried to follow – well, it would just be too bad for them.

Johnny had fallen in with the gang only out of desperation. There had been nowhere else to go at the time. He felt no true loyalty toward them. They were fighting for a lost cause. As for the money, why should he not deserve a share? He had done as much as anyone else had done for it. Looking back, he had probably saved Trace Dawson's life as well at the bank.

At least that was the way Johnny saw it, and at this juncture, the way he saw things was all that mattered.

He had not yet heard the bark of Curt Wagner's Winchester, meaning that the tall man was still stalking a deer. After he had one, gutting it and hauling the meat back to camp would take some time. Now there was only Ben to worry about, and the bald man concerned Johnny only a little. Ben had shown little heart for the fight.

Walking his paint pony back into the outlaw camp, Johnny saw no sign of either Curt or Ben Torrance. Likely Ben had gone to the creek to clean up a little. Crouching, Johnny sorted rapidly through the unsorted stash in the bags. The legal documents he had no use for and tossed them aside. At the bottom of the first sack he found stacks of neatly bundled twenty-dollar notes. Just what he had been looking for. Then his searching fingers came upon two smaller banded sheaves of hundred-dollar bills. Better and better. Reluctantly he left the gold bars at the bottom of the bag alone. He had enough money to make it to Tucson and beyond. To China if he wished to go! Stuffing the loot into his saddle-bags he kept his eyes on the surrounding tangle of brush and trees, watching for any sign of a man approaching, but he saw no one as he swung into his saddle and started the paint pony forward.

Thunder boomed to the north and the clouds there darkened. The wind increased as Johnny Johnson, a rich man now, searched for the southern trail out of the Tanglewood.

By the time Trace Dawson returned to the camp, it had begun to rain. The mounting clouds seemed to have serious intent; the wind was gusting heavily down from the mountain flanks. The horse he rode – Dan Sumner's – was weary and uncomfortable with the rain in its eyes.

No one seemed to be in the camp. Trace's own gray gelding, Curt's dun pony and Ben Torrance's horse were tied to a picket line, shuddering in the cold and rain, so apparently they had not gone far. Trace did notice that Johnny Johnson's black and white paint pony was gone and he frowned as he swung down from the saddle. Maybe Curt had taken it into his own hands

59

to tell Johnny that he was no longer wanted among the gang.

Trace unsaddled, removed the blanket from the back of Sumner's horse, slipped the bit and left it tied to the picket line with the other horses. It was then that a tall figure appeared from out of the lowering mist, toting a deer carcass on his back.

'Damned weather,' Curt Wagner muttered as he let the deer fall free and stretched his weary back. 'It sure set in fast. Well, at least we'll have something to eat for a while.' Curt had been grinning. Now as he looked around the empty camp the smile fell away from his face.

'Where is everyone?' he asked.

'I was just going to ask you the same thing,' Trace said. 'Johnson's pony is gone. I thought maybe you gave him the word to travel on.'

'No, I was going to leave that up to you as we agreed. Is Ben's horse still here?'

'Right where it belongs,' Trace said, nodding toward the picket line.

'Then what—?' It was then that Curt Wagner's eyes fell upon the opened burlap sack, the strewn court documents gathering rain and he cursed slowly, adeptly. 'The kid took something, I'll bet you.'

'You don't think he would have killed Ben? Maybe he got caught in the act.'

'I can't see Johnny doing something like that,' Curt replied. 'But—'

But then, you never knew what a man, a desperate man, would do. 'Let's get to shelter,' Curt said as the rain continued to hammer down, the skies to darken, the wind to increase.

'We have to catch up with Johnny,' Trace argued.

'Where? And how, in this weather? It's impossible even to follow a dry track in the Tanglewood. He could be anywhere.'

As they spoke they rushed to the crude shelter of a tarp tied up between the scrub oak trees of the grove. Sitting on a groundsheet they watched the silver rain pelt the earth, listened to the thunder, winced as close lightning struck, illuminating the skies with momentary brilliance.

'Hell of a bunch of outlaws,' Curt Wagner muttered and Trace had to laugh. 'How is Dan getting along?' Curt asked, and Trace told him about the episode in Lordsberg.

'Well, at least he's got a roof over his head for now. And a bed,' Wagner said miserably.

'Brighten up, Curt,' Trace told his old friend. 'Let's see if we can forage a few dry twigs and boil some coffee while we wait out the storm. Maybe if we put our heads together we can figure out how to proceed from here.'

The thunderstorm had caught Ben Torrance by surprise. He was not a man of the wilderness, and was unable to read the threatening signs of the gathering clouds and rising winds. He had gone to the creek to clean up, crossed it at the shallows, and then he sat on a low sycamore tree limb trying to clear his head, to decide what he should do. This was no life for him, and he knew it. He had sworn allegiance to the gang, but those promises, made when envisioning a better future, were much simpler in the imagination than in the living of them. His vows had come to seem reckless and foolish.

Ben Torrance was no gunman, no roughshod fighting man. He hadn't really believed that Trace, Dan and Curt meant to go through with their plans, but he had wanted to be a party to their hope without actually being involved.

A childish concept, he now recognized. He had gone along primarily, he supposed, because he had nowhere left to go in all the broad West. He had worked and succeeded in making a comfortable life after digging the lone well in the vicinity of Lordsberg. Having congratulated himself on his success, he had forgotten that success is fleeting.

Ben looked up as the thunder racketed down the valleys, sounding like two monstrous beasts butting heads, and lightning crackled. He rose, still without having made a decision, and started back toward the camp, but he had left it too long. The rain began to come down in sudden torrents, veiling his vision. Before he had even reached the river crossing the water had risen, and swollen and furious, the stream rushed between its banks. He could not find the ford he had used earlier.

The cold rain, whipped by the rising wind, fell in confusing swirls, and Ben in sudden panic realized he was not going to be able to cross the river unless he found an easier path. He started downstream.

There the river briefly fanned out and flowed

between thick ranks of cattails and reeds. Screened by the constant rain, the far bank remained hidden. Ben was cold, soaked through. He desperately made his way to the riverbank, and squinting through the steel curtain of the rain, believed he saw a safe way to cross. A small mound of earth rested in the center of the quick-flowing rill and beyond it was a fallen log. If he crossed now, before the water got perilously high, he thought he could make it. Ben eased cautiously from the edge of the creek as the silver rain fell harder.

And stepped into the sucking mud of the bog.

It seemed as if giant hands had reached up to clutch his ankles, trying to drag him downward. Now, pan-icked, he flailed and tried to propel himself more quickly forward, but it was no use. He continued to sink. To his knees, to his thighs. Now half-running, half swimming he knew that nothing he could do was going to save him. He fought violently against the inevitable but found himself sinking lower and lower into the ooze. He screamed, but his throat made little sound above the roar of the water, the rush of the storm, and he simply slid away from life into the depths of the bog.

Johnny Johnson could not find the head of the south-ern trail in the heavy weather. There was a fog across the land and a simultaneous pounding of the rain. The land around him was Tanglewood land: patches of snarled vines and a confusion of interlaced tree branches so tightly packed that they seemed to grow together. He was cold and growing desperate. He gave his pony its head, but the confused animal could find no exit through the mass of dense undergrowth. The wise choice would have been to stop, find some sort of flimsy shelter and sit waiting in the cold for the storm to blow over. But Johnny was a thief and a traitor, running away from his crimes and he thought that when the storm cleared, he might find Curt Wagner and Trace Dawson on his backtrail, wishing to show him a little frontier justice for abandoning the gang. Of course, he considered, as the rain streamed down from his hat brim obscuring vision, the gang itself was a broken concept. There was nothing more to be done against Blakely and Ross; all they had succeeded in doing was to outlaw themselves.

Johnny did not wish to wait around for the law to catch up with them, nor did he wish to face either Trace or Curt Wagner. He knew that either of them was too much man for him to handle.

He could only push on, unsure of his direction, and so he did, forcing his paint pony through the thickest of the briars and brambles and thorny vines, seeking a path out of the Tanglewood.

Fearing that there was none. That once a man entered the Tanglewood, he could never leave.

Dan Sumner rose at the first light of dawn. The storm had broken. Golden sunlight fanned its glow through the scattered remaining clouds. The house was still and cold when he dragged himself from his bed. Kate would have begged him to remain here, he knew. But Dan was suspicious of her father. He thought that perhaps Gentry Cousins had it in mind to turn him over to

Marshal Standish, cutting a deal for himself.

Maybe not, but he was nevertheless putting Kate at risk by staying at the house. What if Kaylin Standish decided to storm the place to capture Dan? He couldn't allow that to happen. There would be gunplay, because Dan would not go along willingly.

And so with the sun barely risen, the shadows deep around the house, Dan slipped through the kitchen door and limped toward the barn. He would have to borrow a horse, but what was one more crime?

He swung the door open and entered to find Kate, dressed in riding clothes, scowling at him.

'I thought so!' she said in sharp accusation. 'Once you've gotten doctored up, you're just going to ride off and leave me?'

'It's not like that, Kate,' he said, going toward her.

'I know,' she said in a kinder voice. 'I know you well enough to guess what's going on in your mind. You didn't want to make more trouble for Father and me.'

'That's about it,' he admitted. 'And I need to get back to the Tanglewood. They'll be waiting for me.'

'For us,' she said definitely and it was Dan's turn to scowl.

'No.' His voice was firm even as he took both of her slender shoulders in his hands and looked into her liquid brown eyes. 'You know what kind of trouble we're in, and you know now what the Tanglewood is like. It's no place for you.'

'No place for a girl?' she jibed.

'That's right – it's no place for a girl.'

'Kiss me.'

'No, I don't think I will,' Dan said, his voice uneven.

'I've got two horses saddled and ready to ride, along with a few sacks of provisions – corn-meal, flour, coffee and beans. If you want them, you'll have to kiss me.'

He did.

The dawn sky still held color as they walked their horses carefully away from the house. Dan feared a shout of alarm; Gentry Cousins would not suffer this lightly, but no cry was raised as they left the grove and found themselves on the long plains, veering north, angling well away from Lordsberg.

The morning was cool, the sunlight scattered, the wind fitful as they guided their ponies toward the Tanglewood. Dan considered simply riding off with Kate to Pueblo or even Denver, giving it all up as a lost cause, but he had given his word to the others, and he knew that even Kate would have thought less of him had he made such a suggestion to her. His face was grim as he rode on; only now and then did he glance at Kate, expecting to see doubt in her eyes, but she was steadfast and occasionally smiled brightly.

It was going to be a rough trail with a good companion.

They came upon the strange rider half a mile from the Tanglewood.

CHAPTER SIX

'Thank goodness!' Ruby Rose Lee said as they drew their horses up beside the dance-hall girl mounted on a pretty little palomino horse. 'I'm damned if I can find a trail in!'

'Why would you want to?' Dan asked, momentarily stunned by Ruby's sudden appearance.

'Why?' Ruby gave a full-throated laugh. 'Ask her,' she said, inclining her head toward Kate Cousins. 'I'm sure she understands. I want to find Trace Dawson. He *is* my man, you know.'

'But Ruby—'

She held up a hand with polished fingernails. 'I know, the Tanglewood is hell. Trace has told me all about it.' The wind shifted a strand of henna-red hair that had freed itself from her man's Stetson across her forehead. 'So is life without him hell. Besides,' she shrugged, 'there's nothing much left for me in Lordsberg, or nothing that I want, not with Gentry Cousins having been forced out of business. The saloon has become a nightly mob scene under Blakely and

Ross. I've had enough. Now I'm taking my last chance at a real life, and that involves my being with Trace.' Her eyes flickered to the other woman. 'You can understand that, can't you, Kate?'

'Fully,' Kate responded firmly, casting a brief glance at the doubtful Dan Sumner.

Dan grumbled, 'Let's get moving then, before someone spots us. Though I don't know how I'm going to explain this all to Trace and Curt.'

'We'll do the explaining,' Ruby said cheerfully, 'you do the guiding.' And the two women drifted their ponies a little away from him to engage in some girl talk as they rode, even chirping a laugh from time to time. Dan led the way gloomily into the depths of the Tanglewood.

With the arrival of morning, Curt and Trace Dawson slipped out of their crude shelter, stretched and looked about them. There was still no sign of Ben Torrance. Johnny Johnson they did not expect to see ever again. It was growing cold, but the sunlight that winked through the trees was bright. It looked like the weather would hold for a while.

'We're going to be in real trouble if we're still up here when the snow starts to fall,' Curt commented.

'That's true,' Trace said to the tall man, 'but we're in a lot of trouble no matter the weather.'

'Have you dreamed up any ideas?'

'On how to proceed – I think so,' Trace said, shaking the coffee pot to see if there was anything left in it.

'Do you mind letting me in on the plan?'

'After we spark this fire to life and heat up the cold coffee,' Trace said. 'Let me get the chill out of my bones and the cobwebs out of my head.'

After the coffee was warmed they stood together, drinking from tin cups. Trace asked Curt Wagner without making eye contact: 'You were going to tell me how you learned the art of cracking a safe.'

'Was I?' Curt looked away and then seemed to shrug off his reticence. After all, Trace was a friend of his now. Curt had a long habit of withholding any and all information. It had kept him out of prison. 'All right,' he said at last, 'you've probably already guessed. I used to ride with an outlaw gang – the Clinch Mountain boys, as a matter of fact.

'I got fed up with it all – the running, the sleepless nights, the prairie hideouts, the internal bickering, the swaggering, the gun fights – I gave it up. Saddled my pony and rode off as far as I could get, looking for a place to settle down and live out my years peacefully.'

'Lordsberg.'

'Yes. Anyway,' he said with a quick smile, 'in my younger years I learned a lot of crafts I had hoped never to use again. I rode a rough trail, but the people here seemed to like me and trust me enough to hang a badge on me. A lot of men take those jobs out of necessity, but I took it because it made me feel wanted, accepted. No more rambling, no more bad companions. I was truly content doing what I did, Trace.'

Trace nodded his understanding. It was about what he had figured. Both men had empty cups now and there was nothing to refill them with. The fire was sizzling out and they tossed the dregs and grounds from the coffee pot and their cups on the fire to help it along its way. They were always cautious with fire. If the Tanglewood ever started to burn there was no rapid escape from the place.

Curt had his head cocked, listening to something. He placed his finger to his lips making a silencing motion to Trace and snatched up his Winchester. Curt pointed to the east and mouthed the word:

'Company.'

Trace, too, reached for his rifle and the two men concealed themselves. Could it be Johnson coming back, or Ben? More likely it was the law looking for them and both men waited with rifles at the ready.

'Hello, the camp!' a familiar voice called out. They recognized Dan Simmer's baritone. A minute later they saw him riding in. There were two people with him.

'I'll be damned,' Trace Dawson said as he stepped forward. Dan had Kate Cousins with him which was not a complete surprise.

But beside her, riding a trim little palomino, was Ruby Rose Lee.

'What is this? A circus?' Curt Wagner said between his teeth.

'I don't know,' Trace replied. But he meant to find out. Just what did Dan have in his mind, bringing the two women into the Tanglewood? Was he going crazy?

That didn't mean that he wasn't pleased to see Ruby, her red hair now drifting free in the wind, her hat on a string down her back. She somehow managed to smell fresh after the long ride and as she strode to Trace and embraced him, her remembered warmth and softness brought a rush of pleasure surging briefly through him. However, he held Ruby away, put a scowl on his face and whirled on Dan who was getting down from leather clumsily because of his injury.

'What the hell is this, Dan!' Trace demanded.

The wounded man shrugged apologetically and answered, 'Trace, I don't know what it is – they said to leave it up to them, they'd explain it to you.'

'Looks like you got yourself bamboozled,' Curt Wagner said, watching as Kate Cousins came up to stand behind her man.

'That doesn't cover it,' Dan Sumner said with a grimace.

'Well,' Curt Wagner said with a grin, 'the gang is getting prettier, but I'm not sure we're gaining any ground.'

Later, then, over the fresh coffee Kate had brought, they had a conference. There was much to be decided. First on the agenda was what to do with the two women. That discussion didn't last long. Both were adamant – they were staying. Kate and Ruby were better at arguing than Trace, and eventually he gave it up.

Ruby had explained her reasons for leaving, saying, 'After Ross and Blakely shoved Gentry Cousins out of the saloon, it started getting rougher and rougher. I thought I had experience with hard men, but then this new crew started drilling in, real hard-cases who even rode roughshod over the town toughs.'

'Where'd they come from?' Trace asked with concern, knowing that Prince Blakely and Ross might very well have imported some killers to track them to the Tanglewood.

'I don't know,' Ruby said sipping at her coffee as she waved a hand toward the sky. 'All over, I guess. They call themselves the Clinch Mountain boys.'

Trace and Curt Wagner exchanged an anxious glance.

'Are you sure?' Curt asked.

'I should be! They proclaimed it loud and clear every time they wanted to start their bragging or scare off the local boys. I had to get out of there. They were plain mean. . . .' Ruby's voice faded as she caught the expressions on the faces of Trace and Curt Wagner.

Ruby asked, 'Why? Do you know something about them?'

'Too much,' Curt muttered, and he rose from the small group and walked away, his coffee cup still in hand.

'What's with Curt?' Dan Sumner inquired.

'I'll tell you later,' Trace said.

'And where are Johnny and Ben?'

Trace told him briefly about Johnny Johnson's rifling the bank loot and disappearing.

'I guess we should have figured that,' Dan said sourly. 'But Ben?'

'Don't know where he is. I'm hoping that Johnny didn't kill him.'

'Johnny has his sneaky side,' Dan answered, 'but I don't think he'd gun old Ben down.'

'I don't either. At any rate,' Trace said with a sigh as he reached for the coffee pot once more, 'that leaves us short-handed. And now Blakely and Ross have the Clinch Mountain boys on their side.' He was thoughtful for a moment, staring into his cup. The wind shifted the brush around them. When he lifted his eyes he said to Dan Sumner, 'Maybe it would be best if you took off for Pueblo, maybe Flagstaff, and took the women with you.'

'I won't go!' Ruby shot out. 'I won't go anywhere without you, Trace. I thought that you had that figured out by now.'

'I'd go if Kate wanted me to, I guess,' Dan said doubtfully, glancing at the small dark-eyed woman at his side. 'I'm still not in much shape for a fight, but – Trace, I wouldn't like it a bit. I don't know if I'd be able to live with myself if I deserted you.'

'We're not going,' Kate Cousins said with quiet firmness.

'But Trace,' Dan asked with doubt still clouding his eyes, 'how long do you mean to keep this up?'

Trace rose to his feet and turned his back to them. Without glancing around, he replied, 'For as long as it takes.' Then he strode away into the dark depths of the Tanglewood.

Curt Wagner returned to the camp before Trace did. He looked worried, but his anger was gone. When he crouched down in front of the small fire he removed his hat and they could see that Curt had taken the time to rinse off and sweep his hair back, combing it with his fingers.

'Did you see Trace?' Dan Sumner asked. Curt just shook his head. He had others things on his mind obviously.

Looking up at Ruby, the tall man asked, 'The Clinch Mountain boys, did you happen to get the name of who's leading them?'

'Sure did,' Ruby said, frowning a little. 'He mentioned it often enough, trying to impress folks, I guess – Cole Lockhart.'

Curt made a small sound deep in his throat that might have been a curse or a murmur of satisfaction. Then he rose.

Dan asked: 'Do you know him, Curt?'

'Yes, I'm afraid I do. I know Cole Lockhart quite well.' Then Curt left them again, walking out into the woods. When he returned this time it was with Trace Dawson. The two sat down on a fallen oak and the others gathered around.

'Trace has been telling me his plan,' Curt Wagner said.

'It's not simple,' Trace said, his eyes narrowing, 'but I see it as our only course. We're not going to hold our own against twenty armed men, that's for sure.'

'Well?' Dan prodded.

'When you kill a rattler, you take off its head and bury it. I mean to go after the head of this bunch.'

'Blakely and Ross?' Kate asked. He nodded at her.

'Prince Blakely, anyway. He's the prime mover. Ross is the money man, the banker; not a man of action. He's indecisive unless it's a matter of finance. I want to remove Blakely.'

'Kill him?' Ruby asked with concern.

'Capture him. Kidnap him, and bring him out to the Tanglewood. With no one to give orders, his little army will soon fall apart.' He paused. 'Or so I hope.'

'What about the Clinch Mountain boys?' Ruby asked. 'They've already been paid, haven't they? That Cole Lockhart doesn't seem like the sort to back down from completing a job.'

Trace spoke carefully, looking at each in turn, 'That's the second part of the plan. We're going to kidnap Cole Lockhart as well.'

Dan almost laughed out loud. 'How are we supposed to do that? A professional gun-for-hire who's always surrounded by his gang of toughs. Blakely, I can see. We simply break into his house and remove him at gunpoint, but Lockhart! How, Trace?'

'I haven't gotten that quite figured out,' Trace was forced to admit. 'The problem, as you say, is getting him away from his gang, putting him in a vulnerable position. We could maybe try sending him a note, drawing him out into—'

'I can do it!' Ruby said emphatically.

'What do you mean?' Trace asked the red-haired woman.

'Don't you believe I can get a man to follow me around the back way to my room? I can play the temptress. Once I have him out in the alley, you could be waiting there to jump him.'

'I won't have it,' Trace Dawson said firmly.

'You said you didn't have a plan,' Ruby insisted. 'I do. And why not? Kate and I are a part of the gang, too. We should start doing our part.'

'I won't have it,' Trace repeated, his expression stony.

'What do you think, Curt?' Ruby asked. 'I'll put on

75

my red dress and sashay around a little. When the time is right, I'll invite Cole Lockhart up to my room, lead him around to the back stairs. You'll be waiting for him.'

'Trace, I hate to say it,' Curt commented hesitantly, 'but it's not a bad plan. Certainly better than trying to come up with some kind of a note to lure him out of the saloon and away from his gang.'

'All right, then,' Trace said with genuine anger. 'We'll put it to a vote.'

Ruby won in the end, and Trace, even though he remained unhappy about the idea, had to admit that it was a workable plan.

If everything went just right.

They were not underestimating Cole Lockhart's skills with weapons, nor his toughness. He had been the leader of the rugged Clinch Mountain boys for a long time without having been challenged. He was good enough and mean enough to make a lot of trouble. Curt, who knew a lot about Lockhart, was well aware of that, yet he thought a drunken Lockhart, alone in the midnight shadows of the alleyway could be taken with just a little planning.

'What about Blakely?' Dan asked. 'Do we try to trick him as well.'

'No, as you said earlier, a couple of us simply knock on his door with our guns drawn. It should be the last thing he'll expect.'

'Should be,' Dan said considering, 'but what if he's hired men to stand watch – or if Marshal Standish has decided to post a deputy there?'

'I don't think they'll have any idea that we'd be riding in there,' Trace answered, 'not with twenty armed men waiting to shoot us down on sight. It's a desperate act, but I've gotten desperate. And tired of losing out to the range pirates.'

They began working on the details of the plan. Ruby was to return to her room and dress for work as if she had never been gone. She hadn't told anyone she was leaving and it was unlikely that anyone even knew that she had been away.

Kate suggested, 'I can go over to the Wabash as well, to help watch out for Ruby. And I could warn you if someone follows Cole Lockhart out the door. No one will say anything. Everyone knows me. I'll just say I need to go into the office to get Father's set of books and check them over. They'll be too busy to care anyway.'

Now it was Dan Sumner who didn't like the suggestion. 'You don't need to get mixed up in this, Kate.'

'I am mixed up in it, Danny,' she said, placing a hand on his shoulder.

'Then I'm going along, bad leg or not,' Dan said firmly. No one tried to talk him out of it.

'Which one do we go after first?' Trace asked. 'Blakely should be the easiest. But you never know.' You never did. Blakely could have hired guns surrounding his house, or Cole Lockhart might manage to draw his belt gun and get off a shot sure to bring the Clinch Mountain boys on the run. Curt Wagner had an idea:

'I say we take Cole first. Sometime after midnight. Then ride to the Blakely house. If Prince Blakely will open the door for anyone at that time of night, it's Cole Lockhart.'

'If we can get Lockhart to go along with the ploy,' Dan said.

'Oh, I think I can convince him to,' Curt said, his expression growing grim. 'He knows I still hold a grudge against him. With the muzzle of my Colt against his back, he'll comply. He knows I'd as soon blow his spine apart as not.'

After Curt and Trace had walked off again, discussing details of the plan, Ruby asked Dan, 'What do you think Curt has against Cole Lockhart?'

'I think,' Dan said, looking toward the Tanglewood where the two men had disappeared up a trail, remembering the angry look on Curt's face, 'that we don't even want to know.'

CHAPTER SEVEN

Ruby sat in front of her mirror in the upstairs room above the Wabash Saloon. Her fingers moved uncertainly as she pinned up her hair. More than once she dropped hairpins on to the floor. She had already changed into her red silk dress. Now she stood, glancing at the mirror as she smoothed her skirt down. This was going to be a dangerous night and she knew it. Still trembling slightly, she took a deep breath and went to the hallway door.

The noise from below hit her like a wall of sound. The Wabash was in full uproar. Men roistering, whooping, banging and cursing. Ruby proceeded to the stairway. She had endured this all before. What was one more night?

She looked straight ahead as she descended to the saloon and crossed the room to sit at the end of the bar. A glance showed her where Cole Lockhart was seated – in a far corner with three other rough-looking men. She did not let her gaze linger on the outlaw chief.

The Clinch Mountain boys had been paid in

advance, and they meant to see how much of it they could spend on cheap liquor. The irony of it was that they were spending their gold in a saloon now owned by Prince Blakely. In effect they were returning their pay to him.

There were two bartenders on duty, both constantly moving to the counter. Abel Hicks, the older of the two gave Ruby a glance, perhaps wondering why she was not out on the floor, hustling drinks and laughing it up with the crude Clinch Mountain boys, but she saw a shadow of sympathy in Abel's eyes as he poured more whiskey for the crowd at the bar.

From where she sat Ruby could also see the seldom-used back door of the Wabash. Now as she glanced that way she saw it open, admitting a wary-looking but determined Kate Cousins. The manager of the Wabash, Zachary Upjohn went to meet Kate. Ruby could not hear their conversation, but it seemed amiable enough.

'Good evening, Kate,' Zachary was saying. He had always liked Kate and Gentry Cousins. The saloon was now making a lot of money, but it was only temporary he knew. When the band of thugs drifted out of town things would return to normal. Zachary did not like the new regime, and he would have drifted on himself except like so many people stranded in Lordsberg, he had no place else to go. Kate used her rehearsed speech.

'Hello, Zachary. I came over to take a look at the books. My father was evicted so suddenly that we didn't have time to do that.'

'I know, and I'm sorry,' Zachary said sincerely. 'Go

on into the office and do what you need to do. Maybe one day we'll be back in business together.'

'I hope so,' Kate said with a fleeting smile. She let herself into the back office, leaving the door ajar, removed two black-bound books from the glass-fronted office book case at random and took them to the desk.

From where she sat, she could see all the way across the crowded saloon to where Cole Lockhart sat getting slowly drunk. And she could see Ruby sitting alone at the end of the bar.

She opened one of the ledgers and stared at the columns of numbers. They had no meaning to her just then. She glanced at the brass-bound wall clock every five minutes, willing the time to fly past, dreading its passage at the same time.

There was death in the air on this night.

Curt Wagner, Dan Sumner and Trace Dawson stood together in the cottonwood grove, staring out at the lights of Lordsberg, from time to time hearing bursts of raucous sound. Dan was uneasy about Kate.

'Shouldn't we be going?'

'Not too soon,' Trace answered. 'We can't chance being seen by some casual observer. That's what happened to you the first time, remember?'

'I remember,' Dan said, rubbing his wounded leg. 'But it's hard to think of the girls down there by themselves.'

'We'll give it another hour,' Trace said, looking to the pointer of the Big Dipper which told him that midnight was still that far off.

'All right,' Dan answered glumly. 'I'll just feel better when I'm doing something. I hate waiting.'

'Dan,' Curt said, going over the plan once again. 'You're the man with one leg, so you'll hold back in the alley with our horses. Stay there unless we need you – if Cole has someone else with him, for instance. Which seems unlikely if he thinks he's going to visit a lady in her room, but who knows?'

'I don't see how Ruby can convince him to take the back stairs.'

'She'll have something made up. The boss doesn't like the girls to be seen taking a man into their rooms – leave that up to Ruby. Kate is in the office near the back door. She'll open it if she sees them leave the saloon. That's our signal to hunker down and get ready.

'Trace, you'll be in the shadows under the back steps, right? I'll position myself behind the loading dock. Men,' Curt said worriedly, 'don't go to shooting unless it absolutely can't be helped. At the first shot we'll have a dozen Clinch Mountain boys on us and the game will be over.'

Shortly before midnight they trailed into town. All three of Lordsberg's saloons were going full-bore. The Black Panther and the Golden Eagle were flush with the displaced Wakapee Valley men who wanted as little to do with the Clinch Mountain boys at the Wabash as possible.

The back alleys of the town, however, were dark and silent for the most part. They passed a few derelict drunks and startled a white mongrel dog into a scuttling run, but other than that they saw no one. Trace had reminded them to be alert for Marshal Standish and his deputies, but these it seemed did not wish to patrol too near to the Wabash at present. Kaylin Standish would not be eager to try stopping any fight that might break out among the Clinch Mountain crowd. For the time being Cole Lockhart's men had taken control of Lordsberg.

Reaching the cross-alley this side of the Wabash, they drew up and Trace and Curt Wagner gave their reins to Dan. Those horses were too well known in Lordsberg. They walked ahead keeping in the shadows which were deep and cold. The moonlight did not reach them between the buildings. Moving only by starlight they found their positions and settled in to wait, their eyes on the back entrance to the Wabash which Kate was supposed to open when Ruby and Cole left the saloon.

If she could.

They knew nothing of the situation inside the saloon, and to Trace it seemed now to be a wildly-hatched plan, based on hope alone. There was no telling what a man like Cole Lockhart would do at any given moment. He took up his position in the deep shadows beneath the stairs which led up to Ruby's room and for the first time since he had started this odds-against war, gave in to despondency.

Ruby knew it was time. What if the men were not in position? Perhaps Kaylin Standish had caught them as they tried to make their way into town. The last thing in the world she wanted was to be trapped alone in her bedroom with the wolfish Cole Lockhart. But she was the one who had suggested it, and the others were depending on her. She rose carefully from her stool at the bar and told Abel Hicks, 'Let me have a tray with four whiskeys for the boys in the corner over there.' She nodded toward the table where Cole Lockhart sat.

Abel Hicks poured them out. He hadn't seen Ruby taking an order from them, but then on this busy night he had little time for observation. Ruby was a longtime employee who knew what she was doing, and so the shot glasses were quickly poured, placed on a tray. Down the bar a bearded man in furs was bellowing for a fresh pitcher of beer. Ruby lofted the tray and started toward Cole Lockhart, her heart pounding.

The easy part was done with.

Ruby put on her most coquettish look, even managing to bat her eyelashes as she approached the table, putting a little additional sway into her walk. *God, I feel like a whore,* she thought. Cole Lockhart looked up at her with slate-gray eyes completely devoid of expression.

'Did we order those?' he asked in a deep voice.

'I figured you were just about ready,' Ruby said with a hint of innuendo.

'I guess so,' Cole said as Ruby unloaded the tray. He did not smile, he did not wink or flirt. Did the man have no emotions at all?

'Mind if I sit with you for awhile?' Ruby asked with concealed urgency. It was growing late; the others would be waiting. If they were to have any chance of succeeding on this night, Cole Lockhart must be susceptible to her feminine allure.

But the man at the table seemed incapable of any sort of feelings.

'Shouldn't you be working?' Cole asked.

'It's my regular night off,' Ruby told him. 'I just wanted the chance to meet you,' she added, trying flattery.

The corner of Cole's mouth twitched. He glanced at his friends who held expressions as stony as Lockhart's.

'Why?' he asked.

'I've heard about you,' Ruby said, smiling like a fool. 'I've been trying to get away from Lordsberg for a long while. I thought—'

'No woman travels with us,' Lockhart said coldly.

'Oh. Well, will you at least give me the chance to wish you a fond goodbye?'

Kate Cousins watched the interplay from the back office. It was rough going for Ruby, she could tell, but although Kate knew little about men, she knew that there were few who could refuse a direct invitation. It was another long fifteen minutes before Cole Lockhart followed Ruby out the front door and Kate leaped from her chair, carelessly placing the ledgers back in the book case.

'Got all you need?' Zachary Upjohn asked as Kate hurried toward the back door.

'I hope so,' she said.

'You know, Kate, I've always had a fondness for you. I was wondering if some time. . . .'

'Yes, sure,' Kate said. She had to crack the back door open to give the signal to the waiting Tanglewood men.

She smiled and sidled past Zachary.

'When?' he persisted.

'Soon, I promise,' she said. 'When this is all over.'

Never had a more false promise been made, but it left Zachary with a smile and allowed her to slip away toward the door.

Curt and Trace, and Dan Sumner who was waiting in the alley with their horses, saw the wedge of light from the opening door. Trace felt his stomach knot up. Cole Lockhart with Ruby. He would not let it happen. No matter their plan, he vowed silently that he would shoot down Cole before he would let that happen.

Trace could not see Curt now. He had hunkered down behind the saloon's loading dock, among the empty beer barrels. The moon had risen high enough so that he could see it over the buildings lining the alley. The stupid white dog had followed along after them and now sat wagging its tail, watching Trace. Great – to have the entire plan spoiled by a mutt! There was no way to shoo the scrawny beast away silently. Cole Lockhart was a cautious man, his vigilance honed by years of watching for the men with badges, noticing the behavior of wild beasts to alert him to lurking hunters.

And now there was that stupid dog, sitting wagging its tail as it looked directly up at Trace concealed in the deep shadows beneath the outside staircase. Trace couldn't even find a rock to toss at it, but even if he had one, hitting it would raise a pained yelp or at least send it scurrying away, and that alone would be enough to raise Cole's suspicions.

He saw them then, rounding the corner in the darkness. Ruby was clinging to Cole's arm and laughing merrily. Trace despised the man at that moment, no matter that it was all a ruse. They had to walk directly past Curt concealed behind the loading dock, and Trace held his breath, but Cole was half-drunk and by now had made up his mind what his evening's entertainment would be and seemed to be totally focused on that.

To Trace's relief, the white dog skulked away in the opposite direction.

Trace braced himself.

Ruby was saying, 'But in Lordsberg, being the small town that it is. . . .'

They were near enough now that by the moon-glow Trace could see a sort of desperate hope in her eyes that belied the cheerfulness of her voice.

'Up there?' he heard Cole Lockhart growl as they neared the steps. Ruby nodded and the outlaw moved ahead, not eagerly it seemed, but warily.

Trace remained crouched in the shadows. He let Cole climb three steps before his hands shot out and took the Clinch Mountain boss by the ankles. Trace yanked – hard – and Cole toppled backward, his head thudding on the lowest step. Cole tried to wriggle free, kicked out violently, but before he could fight his way out of Trace's grip, Curt Wagner was on top of Lockhart.

'Lie still or I'll kill you,' Trace heard Curt threaten.

'You wouldn't – my God, it's you, Wagner. Where—?'

'Shut up and hold still,' Curt growled. 'I'd do it, and

you know it.'

Trace emerged from the staircase and tied Cole's hands behind his back as Curt kept his Colt fixed on Lockhart. Ruby had backed away to stand against the wall of the building, her eyes wide.

'I see you two do know each other,' Trace said to Curt.

'Well enough that Cole knows that shooting him wouldn't leave a blot on my conscience. Better do something to shut him up, Trace. There might be someone around.'

Trace nodded and improvised a gag out of his own and Cole's bandannas.

Yanking their captive to his feet, they walked him along the shadowed alleyways to where Dan Sumner waited with their horses.

'We should have brought an extra pony,' Trace said.

'Couldn't think of everything,' Curt said. 'This way might be better. I'll ride behind Cole with my gun in his back. He can't get up to any mischief that way – not with any hope of surviving.'

Ruby had followed along, obviously anxious.

'What do you want me to do now?' she asked.

Trace told her, 'Wait a half an hour or so and go back into the saloon. If anyone asks about Cole, tell them he fell asleep. Wait a while and then change your clothes and ride back to the Tanglewood, if you can find the way.'

'I think I can now,' Ruby answered.

'Where is Kate?' Dan asked with concern as they swung aboard their horses.

'Still in the office,' Ruby said. 'I'll go in through the back door and tell her what's happened. 'We'll ride back together.'

'Don't wait too long,' Trace advised her. 'Some of the Clinch Mountain boys might decide to go looking for their chief.'

Ruby only nodded her understanding, letting her hand rest on the mounted Trace's leg for a moment before she turned, hoisted her skirts and started away.

'That went pretty well,' Curt Wagner said as they cleared the outskirts of town. In front of him rode a sullen Cole Lockhart. 'Let's hope we have as much luck with the second half of the plan.'

Dan Sumner rode on in silence. He was concerned about Kate Cousins's safety. He still did not see exactly what it was they had accomplished. Perhaps it was like the earlier bank robbery, only a gesture of defiance without real result. Along the road to Prince Blakely's house he began thinking again that it might be wisest to just scoop Kate up and ride away from here.

As far from the Tanglewood as they could get.

CHAPTER EIGHT

There were no lights showing in the white frame house Prince Blakely had built at the edge of town, but then it was well after midnight before they reached it. Hidden behind a stand of old black oak trees, the house was far from imposing, but it remained one of the finest structures in the Wakapee Valley where sawn lumber was still a luxury which needed to be freighted in all the way from Tucson.

Curt Wagner spoke in warning tones to Cole Lockhart as they approached the yard. 'This is what's going to happen, Cole. You and I are going to step up on to Blakely's porch. I'll have my hat tugged down; he won't recognize me in this light. You are going to knock on the door and call out.

'And if you don't go along with us on this – well, you know what the alternative is,' he said, jabbing Cole's spine with the muzzle of his Colt.

Cole Lockhart nodded his head although his eyes were blazing with fury. He would go along with these men for the time being; his time would come to answer this humiliation.

Dan and Trace Dawson remained behind in the shadows of the big oaks while Curt marched Cole Lockhart toward the front porch of Prince Blakely's house. The two men walked so near to each other that the gleam of the metal could not be seen as Curt kept his revolver's muzzle tight against Cole's back. Curt had tugged his hat low to avoid recognition in the moon-light. It was a tense few minutes. Trace and Dan were wary of any sentries that might appear, but none did for the moment.

Trace knocked loudly on the door. Cole still had his hands tied behind him. But his gag had been removed so that he could call out to Prince Blakely. He did and repeated it several times until finally they heard foot-steps approaching the door. Blakely opened the door in his night shirt. He had pulled on a pair of trousers beneath it.

'What in hell?' he stuttered. He recognized Cole immediately. 'Listen, what is this about? If it's more money you want, I don't have it. So far as I can tell there haven't been any results from what I have already handed over. You haven't even found the nest of the Tanglewood gang yet.'

Then his eyes widened as he peered out of the door at the second man standing there. He knew Curt Wagner on sight, of course, and he visibly flinched, backing away toward the interior of the house.

'Cole didn't find us,' Curt said, 'but we sort of found him.'

'What is this?' Blakely sputtered, 'a hold up?'

'Of a sort,' Curt replied as Trace emerged from the shadows, gun leveled, to join them. 'You're going to take a little ride with us.'

Blakely glared at Wagner. 'You were supposed to be a lawman! It's no wonder the town let you go.'

'The town didn't let me go,' Curt replied quietly. 'You did.'

'I suppose that Dan Sumner's in on this, too. What is it you people want with me?'

'Just as I said,' Curt answered, 'to take a little ride with us – you'll like it in the Tanglewood.'

'By God, I'll—!'

'By God,' Curt interrupted sharply, 'you'll tug some boots on and go along with us, or I'll shoot you where you stand. Won't I, Cole?'

'You've been known to,' Cole Lockhart muttered.

'You can't get away with this!' Blakely exploded. 'These criminal acts—'

'Maybe not,' Curt admitted. 'But then, you've been getting away with criminal acts since you moved into the Wakapee Valley, so maybe we can. You never know.'

The small group rode out of Lordsberg, again using a circuitous route. Ruby and Kate had been waiting in the cottonwood grove along the trail. To the relief of Trace and Dan Sumner, both seemed well and in good spirits.

After a glance at the cold-eyed Cole Lockhart and the fuming Prince Blakely, Ruby told them, 'I wasn't so sure I could find my way in the dark, after all. We decided to wait for you.'

'I'm glad you did,' Trace said. 'I would have worried about you all along the trail.'

'Seriously?' she asked.

'Seriously.'

They strung out along the road then, Trace leading the way with Lockhart behind him, watched closely by Curt Wagner. Then came Prince Blakely whose complaining had died to an occasional murmured threat. Dan Sumner, riding side by side with Kate Cousins, trailed.

'Thanks for showing me the road in,' Cole said to Curt. 'I was wondering how I was going to find the way.'

'No point in you learning the way,' Curt said with a naked threat. 'You're never going to get out of the Tanglewood alive.'

Cole Lockhart, astonishingly, laughed out loud, drawing all eyes to him. 'You're a lot of things, Curt, but I don't believe you'd ever kill a man in cold blood.'

'We'll find out, I expect. Don't forget Cole, I learned everything I know from you. And I wouldn't expect any help from the Clinch Mountain boys. They'll never find the way unless you're leaving a trail of bread crumbs.'

'What are you talking about?' Prince Blakely asked angrily.

'Curt is given to flights of fancy,' Cole said. 'Like thinking he's on some crusade as he apparently does now.'

'I place the blame on your lap,' Prince Blakely said and Cole gave him a sneer in return.

'Place it where you want, fat man. You can't believe that I care one way or the other.'

93

Trace led the way through the dense thickets, winding this way and that in a way that seemed pattern-less to Blakely. He, too, had been trying to memorize the way in through the Tanglewood to the outlaws' camp, but in the darkness he became totally disori-ented and finally gave it up, riding along in silent confusion.

The Tanglewood had a way of impressing people that way.

Dark, overgrown, tangled and desolate. Even by moonlight, Blakely could not see the trail their horses were following. The overhead, intertwined boughs of the trees cut off most of the glow of the golden light cast by the fading moon. Life became a shadow without the faintest glimmer of light. In the Tanglewood, Blakely could see his own hopes for a bright future fading to darkness as well. All of his money wouldn't buy his way out of this primitive landscape, this evil place.

'You must do something!' Storm Ross was shouting at Marshal Standish.

'Do you have a suggestion?' the lantern-jawed man said from behind his desk. Dawn had only just arrived, spreading a faintly reddish sheen across the walls and floor of the marshal's office. 'Besides, you never trusted me to do anything before. Isn't that why you brought in the Clinch Mountain boys?'

'That's just the thing!' the narrow banker shrilled. 'The Tanglewood gang somehow snatched Cole Lockhart from under their very noses. Bunch of drunken pigs!' he flared.

'That's what you hired; what did you expect?' Kaylin Standish asked, momentarily basking in the glow of his suddenly resurgent reputation.

'And they got Prince Blakely! What sort of law officer are you, anyway?'

'The kind who can't be everywhere at once,' Kaylin said, rising to stretch and momentarily go to his open office door to watch the sunrise over Lordsberg. 'I told you that bringing in all of that extra help was useless. You could send an army into the Tanglewood and they would have little success finding those boys.'

'Maybe so,' Storm Ross said, calming a little. 'The question is – what do we do now?'

'I don't know exactly. We could maybe offer a reward, though that hasn't done much good in the past. Or,' Kaylin Standish said tentatively, 'we might offer an amnesty.'

'What?'

'Offer them – Trace and Curt Wagner, Johnny Johnson, Ben, all of them – an opportunity to surrender with the promise of no charges being filed against them. Of course,' Standish said, 'we'd throw them all in the lock-up the minute they appear.'

'That's devious.'

'Is it not? Have you any better suggestions?'

'How about this Gentry Cousins? His daughter is supposedly riding with the gang. I could agree to let him have control of the Wabash Saloon back if he tells us where the gang is. She's his only child; surely she'll be in contact with him sooner or later.'

'That'll mean giving up Dan Sumner. Kate would never do that,' said Kaylin, who knew more about local affairs than Ross.

'Who's Sumner?' asked Ross, who was little involved in Blakely's machinations.

'Young man who was trying to scratch out a living on a Pima Creek homestead, up near the Wakapee River. He wanted to get Kate out of her father's saloon and the life there.'

'I see,' Ross said impatiently as if the lives of the two young people had no interest for him. 'Well, why don't we take that thought of yours and make it a little more restricted and productive? We could promise this Dan Sumner complete amnesty.' Ross's eyes brightened. 'And tell him if he comes in, we'll even offer a reward for the location of the others, and the recovery of the bank money.'

'He won't go for that,' said Marshal Standish, who knew Dan well enough.

'For the sake of his lover?' Ross asked. 'And she for the sake of her father? I think it might work, Marshal.'

'You know what, Mister Ross,' Kaylin Standish replied after giving it some thought, 'so do I. Let's go out and have a talk with Gentry Cousins.'

'You know, Dan,' Kate Cousins was saying as they sat in a thorny bower of mesquite and blackthorn, sheltering from the sun, trying to swat away a virtual cloud of gnats that had decided to join them there, 'I can't help but worry about my father.'

'That's understandable,' Dan said as he waved his

hand in front of his face where the swarm hovered. There was a breeze blowing, but it did nothing to keep the flying insects down, and little to cool them. Cold at nights, sweltering in the daytime, the Tanglewood offered no compromise. Curt Wagner had killed a five-foot rattler that morning when it slithered through their camp as he took his turn standing watch over Cole and Prince Blakely.

'We'll get through this, though. We have bargaining chips now.'

'I suppose,' Kate said with a sigh, 'but I can't help feeling that I've abandoned Father when he needed me the most.'

'What do you want to do?' Dan asked with deep concern. He couldn't risk losing Kate now. Now that he was sure he wanted her always to be at his side. Earlier in their relationship it might have just been mutual attraction or the impulse of the young that drew him to her, but now he knew that she was becoming the woman he always wanted – one who would stand by her man and fight for him. He couldn't stand it if she ever left him.

'I think I should see him. With the loss of the Wabash and of his darling daughter, he must be feeling desperate. I just want to assure him that I'm all right – and that you will take care of me,' she said, gently kissing his cheek.

'Outlaw that I am,' Dan muttered.

'Outlaw that you are.' Kate rose, stretched her arms over her head and looked down at Dan. 'So, what do you think?'

'I understand your sense of obligation, Kate, but there are more than just two of us whose lives are at stake here. What if Marshal Standish, or worse, the Clinch Mountain boys, managed to trail you back into the Tanglewood?'

'I would see anyone and lay a false trail,' Kate told him.

Dan was silent, seeing the intent in Kate's eyes. There were different sorts of responsibility. 'I'd have to talk to Trace and Curt.'

'This isn't a prison,' Kate said with a little heat.

'In a way it is. I have at least to let them know what you have in mind. It's risky for everyone.'

Cole Lockhart sat with his hands free, his ankles tied, near the tiny campfire as Trace and Curt Wagner sipped coffee. Cole drank from his own tin cup, seated on the ground near a brooding Prince Blakely. He watched as Ruby, who had changed back into range clothes, perched on a fallen log. His eyes were malevolent as he said, 'You're a deceitful little thing, aren't you?'

'Yes, I guess I am. And proud of it,' Ruby replied.

'This will only mean more trouble for all of you,' Blakely tried.

Trace laughed out loud. 'How in hell could we be in more trouble!'

'When I get you back to Lordsberg, Judge Weems will—'

He was cut off by Curt Wagner. 'Do you mind telling me how you plan to do that?' he asked.

'You can't stay forted up in this godforsaken place

forever. You have to come out one day!'

'I suppose we will,' Curt agreed. 'What makes you think that you'll be around to go with us, Blakely?'

'Why, because I—' Blakely sputtered. But suddenly he realized that he had no idea what these men were capable of. He had taken away their property and destroyed their lives. Why would they not strike back with even more viciousness? He fell to silence and sipped at his coffee as a stream of fire ants passed over his bound ankles.

'If they bite, you'll feel it forever,' Trace said. 'Their jaws come out in your flesh and stay there.'

If there was a message there, Blakely didn't get it, but no one made a move to help him shift his position or drive the ants away. That alone was symbolic.

Johnny Johnson was breathing easier although the sun across the open white desert was fierce even at this time of the year. It might be snowing in the high mountains, but the long flats were sweltering. He figured that he had angled out of Colorado some time ago, and his direction must have taken him into Arizona. There he meant to reach either Tucson or Phoenix in a few days and live a life of luxury not concerning himself with trivial matters like water. He sipped at his canteen. The water in it was tepid.

He saw no settlements ahead across the long desert, but far to the south a dark figure seemed to be approaching on horseback. Small and indistinct, whoever the traveler was, he might be able to point Johnny in the right direction, could even know of a pueblo nearby where he could rest and water his horse, spend some of the money in his saddle-bags on a plate of good Mexican food, *cerveza*, and waste some on the company of a dark-eyed woman. He let his paint pony drift that way, and within the hour he drew up to wait for the traveler.

'Hello, Johnny,' the lone rider said.

'Do I know you?'

'Unless you've got a short memory,' Laredo answered, and now Johnson did recognize the lean hawk-eyed man.

'Laredo, listen. . . .'

'You are going to have to listen, Johnny. You've got a good sense of direction. You told me the other day that I was in Colorado and couldn't arrest you. This is Arizona Territory. You'd be surprised at how much latitude I've been given to arrest bank robbers here.'

'I've never even been in Arizona before, let alone robbed a bank!' Johnny protested loudly, but weakly.

'I've explained all this to you before. We have a reciprocal agreement with Colorado. Don't test me. What they might do with you is up to the judges. The Bank Examiner's office has given me the authority to investigate and arrest anyone suspected of bank robbery.'

Johnny's paint pony shifted its feet uneasily. He kept his eyes fixed on Laredo, not liking what he saw in those eyes.

Laredo folded his hands on his saddle pommel and made a suggestion. 'You can take the loot back, Johnny. Or hand it over to me and I'll do it.'

'I can't go back to Lordsberg,' Johnson said, realizing belatedly that he had just admitted to theft. He added in a more subdued voice, 'And I can't go back to the Tanglewood – Curt and Trace will be furious with me. Not only for taking what I did, but for what they'll view as cowardice.'

'You don't have a lot of options, Johnny. I could take you back to Tucson with me, but they have a nasty habit of hanging bank robbers in that town.'

Johnny's Adam's apple bobbed up and down. The wind was dry; his throat was parched. Laredo did not look like he was fooling.

'I guess,' he said hesitantly, 'I could just give it to you. If you wouldn't. . . .'

'I only want to see justice done. I don't get any pleasure out of seeing young men swinging from the gallows,' Laredo said. Although he had sent a few that way himself, he was serious. Johnson was only a very young man who had once thought he could make his way in the West, been thwarted and then had temptation put in his way. He was not a criminal in the true sense of the word, unlike a few that had crossed Laredo's path.

'If I hand over my saddle-bags, there won't be any charges filed against me?' Johnny asked, bargaining.

'That's just not up to me, Johnny. I don't know, but from what my investigators have told me about the method of operation at Storm Ross's bank, I'd say no one will have much time to be worrying about your part in this.'

'All right, then,' Johnson said, untying his saddle-bags. 'Take the money and be damned!' He paused. 'I don't suppose I could keep at least twenty dollars for a meal and for my horse's feed.'

Laredo's mouth twitched. 'I can't let you do that but' – Laredo fished in the pocket of his jeans – 'I can loan you twenty.' And he slipped a twenty-dollar gold piece, bright in the sun, to Johnny. 'Just stay out of trouble. You may be getting back your ranch in the Wakapee after this is all over. That's not a promise, but it's the way our legal people see it working out.'

'All right.' Johnny's tough expression had softened. 'Thanks, Laredo. Do you happen to know of a pueblo nearby where I can get a decent meal?'

'About five miles ahead, there's a place called Los Coches. Ask for a restaurant named La Paloma – tell Maria that I sent you. She'll treat you right.'

Laredo smiled, fitted the saddle-bags over his own and then turned his big buckskin horse northward. There was still much to do.

Johnny Johnson watched the man ride away. Laredo had given him hope for the future; perhaps he could get his little horse ranch back now. And, he reflected, it had to be a better life than becoming an outlaw on the run.

CHAPTER NINE

'I have to go back with her,' Dan Sumner was saying. Curt and Trace Dawson both were eyeing him uneasily. They were not quite scowling, but their expressions were the next thing to it. To Dan just now, Trace knew, the woman's needs were more important to him than caution. It had backfired the last time.

'It will require extreme caution,' Curt warned as they stood together apart from the prisoners who seemed to have their ambitions toward escape beaten down by the torpid weight of the day.

'I know that,' Dan answered, wiping his sleeve across his sweaty brow. 'But we've all taken more than a few chances already.'

'If you feel like you have to do it, then go along,' Curt Wagner said, not angrily but with a sort of regretful understanding. They couldn't have held him back anyway. Dan Sumner walked away toward the horses where Kate waited. His limp was not as noticeable as it had been.

'Can't blame a man for wanting to do something for

the woman he loves,' was Trace Dawson's comment.

'No – Trace, I think the time has come to move our camp,' Curt responded.

'Do you have a place in mind?'

'I think so. Up along a ledge near the bat cave. I can't see how anyone could approach us there without our seeing them.'

Trace nodded. He agreed with Curt, but it seemed that every move they made took them farther into the Tanglewood. Yet the Clinch Mountain boys would eventually come looking for them and Kaylin Standish might gather enough courage to do the same with enough prodding. Undoubtedly Storm Ross would have made his plea to the marshal to rescue Prince Blakely, the driving force behind the land takeover. And he would have offered incentives. The sensible thing for them to do was to go deeper into the Tanglewood. Deeper into the nightmare.

'What are you thinking?' Curt asked, studying his friend's troubled face.

'Just how smart we are,' Trace grumbled. 'Do we tell Dan now where we're going?'

'What do you think?'

'Dan would never give us up – voluntarily. But let's do it while he's gone. We can keep an eye out for his return.'

'I agree,' Curt said with some relief. They had no more assaults on Lordsberg planned. From here on it would become a defensive battle.

'Coming in!' a strange, yet somehow familiar voice called out, and both men spun, reaching for their revolvers. Curt, squinting into the sunlight, was the first to recognize the man. He gestured to Trace to holster his gun as Laredo entered their camp.

'How'd you find us from the south?' Trace asked honestly surprised. 'Were you brought up in this area or something?'

Laredo laughed. He sat his big buckskin horse, watching them closely. 'My horse smelled your animals, and your voices carry a lot farther than you'd think in the silence of the place. I just started following the tracks that Johnson left going out of here, and there you were.'

'Did you see Johnny?' Curt asked with a hint of disgust.

'He asked me to return these,' Laredo said, untying Johnson's saddle-bags from behind his saddle and simultaneously swinging down to stand before Curt and Trace. 'He said he'd changed his mind about keeping what he took.'

Both outlaws looked dubiously at Laredo, but the money had been recovered – money they had never meant to keep, but only to hold as a threat over the heads of Blakely and Ross.

Curt Wagner watched as Laredo unsaddled his horse and asked, 'Mind if I ask where you've been?'

'Trying to clear up the legal side of things,' Laredo said. 'I see you've taken a different tack.' He nodded toward the camp where Prince Blakely and Cole Lockhart sat with their feet tightly bound.

'We had to make a move,' Trace said tightly.

'You boys make a lot of moves without thinking them

through,' Laredo said, throwing his saddle to the ground. 'The courts might have straightened this all out, given time.'

'Given time and an honest judge!' Trace shouted in exasperation. 'We didn't feel like we had either.'

'I understand that, believe it or not,' Laredo replied. 'I've set the wheels in motion for you. If you can avoid acting criminally any more you just might get out of this with minimal damage.'

Trace was still too angry to answer civilly. He turned his back and went to look for Ruby.

Curt, a little calmer, said, 'Thank you, Laredo.'

From the camp, Blakely who had heard bits and pieces of the conversation said plaintively, 'Are you a lawman? Get us out of here!'

Laredo took three steps that way, looking into the desperate eyes of Blakely and the cold, cold eyes of Cole Lockhart.

'I'm not exactly a lawman. I work for the Bank Examiner's enforcement arm in Arizona. Our investigators and accountants have a few questions for you and Mr. Ross. I don't have the authority in Colorado to detain or free you. I suppose if you wanted to ride with me voluntarily to Tucson to talk to our legal people, that could be done.'

'Go to hell,' Prince Blakely said.

'That's about what I expected you'd say,' Laredo said. 'Let's just all wait and see how this plays out.'

'Who's he?' Kate Cousins asked Dan in a hiss as they trailed out of camp.

'To tell you the truth, I'm not exactly sure,' Dan

answered. 'Something to do with the banking business.'

'Sure doesn't look like any banker I've ever met,' she commented.

'No. He's something like a lawman hired to track down people who rob banks – or misuse them. I'm just thankful that he seems to be on our side.'

Laredo settled in between the two groups remaining in the camp – Trace, Curt and Ruby on one side, the disgruntled Prince Blakely and Cole Lockhart on the other. He had a tin cup containing coffee in one hand. He was surrounded by mistrustful eyes which was not a new experience for him.

He thought briefly back to the beginning of his long, sometimes fruitful, always hazardous career.

Once, a long time ago, Laredo had found himself down and out. He had been eyeballing a bank in a small town called Cannel, Arizona Territory. Laredo was hungry, tired and broke. While he stood considering the bank as a solution to his troubles, a man who moved on cat feet slipped up beside him in the hot shade of the alleyway and introduced himself.

'Jack Royle's my name,' he said, stuffing the bowl of a stubby pipe with tobacco.

'Pleased to meet you,' Laredo replied shortly. He was not in the mood for a stranger's idle conversation.

'Working in town, are you?' Royle persisted, lighting his pipe.

'Not at the moment.'

Royle nodded, blew out a stream of tobacco smoke and studied the tall stranger. 'I, myself, am employed

107

here,' he said. Laredo cast an annoyed glance at the stocky man. 'For the present, that is. I travel all around,' Royle continued, indicating all of the territory with a wave of his pipe.

'What are you, some kind of drummer?' Laredo asked.

'No. I am employed, my young friend, as an operative in the enforcement arm of the Territorial Bank Examiner's office.'

'Oh.' Laredo felt cornered suddenly. The inoffensive little man stood watching him quietly. Laredo wondered how Royle could have known what he had in mind that hot, dry, desperate day.

'Yes,' Royle went on, 'you know men will try to stick up these little banks in isolated areas. Then they make their break toward Mexico, California, anywhere, free as birds. The local law doesn't have the time or the resources to expend hunting them down. Me,' Royle said with a gnome-like smile, 'I've got all the time in the world. All the time in the world.' With that the little man nodded and walked away. Laredo stood watching his back. If that had not been a warning, it was the next thing to one.

It wasn't until late afternoon that Laredo traced Royle to his hotel room where he sat shirtless, bare feet propped up.

'Mr Royle,' Laredo had said, 'how's chances of getting hired on at a job like yours?'

That had been long ago, and many miles past, pursuing bank robbers and evildoers, some of them apparently solid citizens in town suits, lining their pockets with the money earned by the sweat of the brow of their hard-working, honest depositors. Laredo found that he disliked these criminals much more than the thugs that kicked in the door of a bank with guns flashing. If what Cassidy and Stolz – the two clever money-men at the home office – suspected, could be proven true, Blakely and Ross had stolen the property and the hopes of dozens of young families in the Wakapee Valley.

Blakely disgusted Laredo. In a way so did Cole Lockhart, but he at least did not present himself to be other than he was: a killer for hire.

Laredo had never before encountered the Clinch Mountain boys, although he knew them by reputation. Perhaps the reason he had never crossed their path was that they had never been implicated in anything like a bank robbery. They were quite simply a roving band of thugs, guns for hire. Just now, however, he did take the time to memorize Cole Lockhart's face. The roads the two men followed seemed likely to cause them to collide sometime in the future.

Curt Wagner who remained cooler than the angry Trace Dawson asked, 'You think there's a hope we can get our property back, do you, Laredo?'

'That's what the Bank Examiner seems to think. There was lot of discussion about homesteading, prior claims and assumed ownership couched in legal terms I didn't really understand, but the way it was explained to me, based on the documents I provided them, they are tending to believe that the Ross-Blakely power play was nothing less than a land-grab. They're also looking into the background of Judge Weems.'

Blakely had been listening intently to all of this and sat sullenly in the heat of the Tanglewood, his face a mask.

'Did they tell you how long it might take to resolve all of this?' Trace asked, still obviously agitated.

'It will be a while, since Colorado and Arizona are both involved. They'll have to communicate and settle matters of jurisdiction. I couldn't give you a good guess as to how long it will actually take.'

'All we have to do is keep ourselves from being hanged in the meantime and we might come out of this all right,' Trace said with a hint of sarcasm.

'It's more hope than we had before, Trace,' Curt reminded him.

'Yes – we've advanced from none to slim.'

'What do you think we can do, Laredo?' Curt asked the visitor.

'I can't see anything but what you've been doing – hole up until this is done with, one way or the other.'

'Doomed to life in the Tanglewood,' Trace said.

'It's a life. Where there's life, there's hope. Isn't that what they say?'

'That all depends on what kind of life you have,' Trace muttered, and he spun on his heel and stalked away.

'I don't think the man has much faith in the authorities,' Laredo said.

'Would you?' Curt asked. 'After what we've been through?'

'I guess not,' Laredo had to admit. He got to his feet

now and told Curt, 'I have to have the loot – to return it to the bank. It's part of the deal I made for you men. Our job is to recover bank funds that are stolen and punish those who take them. I have no authority to make an arrest in Colorado, as I've already told you, but still I have an obligation to recover the money in any way that I can.'

'I'd have to talk to Trace,' Curt answered slowly. After all, they did not really know who Laredo was. Maybe he was just a smooth-talking con man.

'Do that,' Laredo said, resting his hand on his stag-handled revolver. 'But try to convince him that it's easier for everyone if I take it into Lordsberg. You don't need it to bargain with now. You've got them,' he said, inclining his head toward Cole and Blakely.

'Why don't you free us, too?' Blakely asked with a sense of desperation. Laredo didn't even bother to answer.

'I've got Johnny Johnson's cut – now I need the rest of it, Curt. It will make things easier on all of you and speed up the process.'

'I'll tell Trace.'

'I'll also need a pack animal to carry the gold.'

'Take his horse,' Curt said, his eyes drifting savagely to Blakely. 'He won't be needing it.'

'Where will you be when I get back?' Laredo asked.

'In a different camp. But why ask? You seem to be able to find us no matter where we are.'

'That's a part of my job,' Laredo said with a faint smile. 'You should hope that the men looking for you don't have a really good Indian tracker with them.'

Now Curt glanced at the leader of the Clinch Mountain boys, but Cole's face was unreadable. Lockhart said in an icy voice: 'They'll find me sooner or later, Wagner; you can bet on that, and when our situations are reversed, I'll show you some Clinch Mountain justice.'

Laredo had stepped away to prepare his buckskin horse for travel once more. He had no need to hear the men exchanging threats. They were always the same. His only concern was the legalities involved. His new boss, Deacon Cody, who had taken over from an ailing Jack Royle, had told him that things would go smoother all around and probably easier on the Tanglewood gang if he could get them to surrender the stolen money.

Laredo saddled Prince Blakely's unremarkable bay horse which seemed to be a retired army mount, probably purchased on the cheap. Prince didn't do or want to do much riding. Having the saddle on made it easier to tote the burlap bags which could be tied to the saddle horn. The sacks containing the gold were heavy, but nothing a moderately healthy horse would be severely burdened by.

Curt had returned to watch Laredo as he finished loading the horse.

Laredo glanced at the tall man and asked, 'Did you talk to Trace?'

'I did,' Curt said a little unhappily.

'And?'

'He said, "Take it and be damned".'

'I wouldn't expect him to say much else. You men

risked a lot to get it. But tell Trace for me that this is the right thing to do. It will make it easier for the law to sort things out and might save you all some prison time.'

'I guess we'll have to trust you, Laredo,' Curt responded. 'The money wasn't doing us any good sitting around here, anyway. The robbery was just another idea gone wrong.'

'You understand, Curt,' Laredo said, tying a knot in his saddle rope. 'That's the point of it – you men didn't flee with the money when you could have. You never meant to spend it at all. An honest judge might be able to understand your motivation when all the facts are revealed.'

'I hope so,' Curt said, turning away. Then he asked, 'You say you met Johnny Johnson on the trail in?'

'I did. He's all right – waiting to see if he can get his horse ranch back.'

'I'm glad to hear it. I always liked the kid, till he pulled that stunt.' Curt walked away through the shadows of the Tanglewood.

Laredo lingered long enough to refill his canteens at the creek. Then he crossed the camp again and swung heavily into leather. His spurs chinked slightly as he touched them to the buckskin's flanks with just enough force to let the big horse know that it was time to move on.

Laredo found the head of the trail easily enough and though the road itself was a labyrinth, it had been ridden enough lately that he could easily follow it by using the tracks he saw. Curt was right about it being time to move their camp. They had been marking the trail in too distinctly.

If a day can be hot and cool at the same time, this one was. In the shadows the wind rolling down from off of the Rockies was chilling, but in the areas sheltered from the wind where the sun shone, the high sun was hot on Laredo's back. It was, although Laredo did not know it, typical Tanglewood weather.

Following the switchbacks of the trail through head-high brush, he eventually emerged on to the flats. Clearing the chaparral, he saw two riders far ahead of him angling toward Lordsberg. He recognized their horses even at that distance. Dan Sumner and Kate Cousins. Now what were those two doing riding toward town?

This was no time for unexpected complications. Worriedly, Laredo rode on as the sun glared down and the long wind blew across the plains.

CHAPTER TEN

The bank was already open for business when Laredo reached Lordsberg, leading Blakely's laden horse, but there was little activity. The teller, in fact, was standing in shirt sleeves, arms crossed, in the sunlit doorway. Laredo called out to him.

'You! Do you work here?' He got a surly nod in response. Laredo said, 'Call Storm Ross out for me, would you? We've some business to conduct.'

'You could go in yourself,' the man said, with some truculence.

'No, I can't,' Laredo said. 'I don't think it's a good idea to leave all this gold out on the street.'

'What gold?' the man asked, approaching slowly, his eye narrowed.

'The bank's money!' Laredo said, his irritation with the teller now showing. 'Just get Ross and tell him I've brought back the stolen money.'

'Maybe I'd better get the marshal,' the man said.

'Maybe you'd just better get Ross,' Laredo replied, and now his growing anger was clear enough.

The sullen man disappeared into the bank and a minute later Storm Ross himself appeared, his face a mixture of expressions: doubt, disbelief, hope, fear. At his shoulder stood a large bearded man. One of the Clinch Mountain boys, Laredo guessed.

'What's this about you having the bank's money?' Ross asked.

'It's there, tied on to the bay.'

'That's Prince Blakely's horse!' Ross said, growing excited.

'Yes, it is. I borrowed it from him.'

'You're one of them, then – one of the Tanglewood bunch,' Ross said, and the man beside him unbuttoned his coat, revealing a businesslike Colt revolver.

'No, I'm not,' Laredo said. 'Do you want this gold and currency or not? I don't like conducting business in the street.'

'Swing down; come in. Let's get the bags inside, Leo.'

The big man, Leo, went to the side of the bay horse and began untying the heavy sacks.

'Are all of our documents in there too?' Ross wanted to know.

'Most of them,' Laredo said, getting down from the saddle. 'Except the ones I gave to the Bank Examiner's office.'

'What are you talking about?' Ross asked, paling a little. 'Which papers?'

'A few disputed land claims, a few foreclosure papers.'

Ross's eyes narrowed further. 'Who are you?' he asked squinting into the brilliant sunlight.

'I told you that I don't like doing business in the street. If we can go into your office, I'll tell you, and we can discuss matters.'

Ross looked around confused, then he called to his teller, 'Tipton, come out here and help Leo unload this horse and bring everything into the bank!'

They walked past the tellers' cages, Ross running a harried hand over his head. They entered a small, cool office where Ross offered Laredo a chair but did not sit down himself. The little man's mind was obviously furiously at work, speculating on what all of this meant.

'All right, then,' the banker said, leaning against the wall and folding his arms which he apparently thought was adopting a casual stance but which only made him look more nervous than ever, 'let's hear what you have to say.'

Behind Laredo heavy steps approached and the burlap bags, one by one, were dropped on to the floor of Ross's office. Glancing that way Laredo saw that the teller, Tipton, had scurried away, but Leo lingered near the door.

Laredo leaned back in his leather chair and began. He told Storm Ross who he was, what authority he had and did not have, and some of what he had done to recover the money.

'Is this some sort of blackmail scheme!' Ross demanded after Laredo had summed up. 'Are you trying to buy the freedom of the Tanglewood outlaws?'

'No. My mandate is only to return stolen bank property. The rest is up to the legal people. You aren't in a much better position right now than the Tanglewood crowd is, you know.'

'What do you mean?' Ross was growing angrier, more frustrated.

'Once my superiors and the people from Denver have had their meeting, someone will be coming to examine your books very closely.'

'Ask him where the Tanglewood gang is hiding out,' Leo growled from the doorway. 'He knows. How else could he have gotten the money back along with Blakely's horse.'

Ross ignored the bearded man for the moment. His brow was furrowed with concern. He knew full well that he and Blakely had hijacked the property they now held – half of the Wakapee Valley – and that their methods had been outside the law. It could be that he was watching everything he owned trickle away. He tried another ploy.

'I should have you arrested,' he said to Laredo.

'For returning the bank's money?' Laredo asked innocently.

'For conspiring with criminals, withholding information in a criminal inquiry, for—'

'Go ahead,' Laredo said. By now he was used to being threatened. He was no lawyer himself, but his powers and limits to them were carefully and precisely outlined. He worked for the Bank Examiner's office; his responsibility began and ended with protecting the banks in his region. No one expected him to charge headlong into a battle with a bunch of desperadoes, not when there was the more reasonable approach of simply asking them to return the stolen goods which they had never intended to keep in the first place.

Laredo told Ross, 'It would just bring my boss and his accountants up from Tucson more quickly.' He added, 'Then, of course, I would have to bring a charge of false accusations against you.'

'There must be a way out of this,' Ross said as if he himself were approaching the idea of blackmail.

'Sure there is. Relinquish your claims to the Wakapee Valley land you've confiscated, give Gentry Cousins's saloon back to him and try running an honest bank for the people of Lordsberg.'

'You don't understand! Blakely—'

'I do understand. Blakely is a land pirate. You got yourself tied up with the wrong man. Maybe you got a little too greedy, I don't know, but it's not too late to cut loose and run your business as you know it's supposed to be run.'

'I want to know where the Tanglewood bunch is hidden out,' Leo persisted, his one-track mind determined. 'You've got Cole Lockhart up there, too, don't you? I don't know how you managed to take him, but I know you have him.'

'*I* don't have anybody captive anywhere,' Laredo answered. 'You'll have to find him yourself, if he's there.'

'You'll tell me, damnit!' Leo flared, and to Ross's surprise and to Laredo's, the big man decided to make a move. He grabbed Laredo's collar and tried to pull him bodily out of the chair he was sitting in.

Laredo slapped the meaty hand away, came to his feet and braced himself. Like ninety per cent of the street brawlers in the world, Leo's idea was to land a solid right-hand punch and knock Laredo down if not out. Laredo blocked it easily and drove his own right hand into Leo's flabby waist just above his belt buckle. Leo staggered back, bent over, struggling for breath.

'That won't get you far, Leo,' Laredo warned the big man as he crouched, bunching his fists, and started to come in again. Storm Ross made a small squeaking sound as Leo again tried to drive his huge right fist against Laredo's jaw, again had it blocked, again took an answering blow from Laredo's right, this one on his ear which began to bleed. Leo backed away as Laredo set his shoulders and began peppering the man's face with left jabs. Three in a row caught Leo on the nose, on his right eye. Ross squeaked again and Laredo glanced at the banker to assure himself that the little man had no idea of joining in. He did not.

And it seemed that Leo had about had enough. His back went up the wall beside the doorframe with a heavy thump and Laredo saw his hand move toward his holstered revolver. He warned Leo, 'That won't get you far either, Leo,' and Laredo's hand flicked down and slicked his stag-handled Colt from its oiled holster, his thumb ratcheting back the curved steel hammer of the weapon.

The hardened outlaw seemed stunned. His hands flinched as if he meant to raise his arms, but his pride gave him second thoughts. He looked as if he wanted to go for his pistol again, but he was looking down the barrel of a cocked and leveled .44 revolver, and even Leo knew that he had no chance in that situation.

'I told you before, if you want Cole Lockhart, you'll have to find him yourself,' Laredo said, 'but I'm warning you – there are twenty men up in the Tanglewood who are tougher than I am.'

'This isn't the end of this,' the outlaw said in that sullen way that men use when they mean that it is the end, but need just a bit of pride to cling to. Then he turned heavily toward the front door of the bank, leaving Laredo and Ross alone again.

Looking steadily at the banker, Laredo told him, 'I don't have much more to say to you, Ross, but you need to think about changing the way you do business.'

The small man said quietly. 'I have been. I've been thinking about things for a long time. I was with Blakely because – well, he knows how to shake the money tree. But things have gotten out of hand.'

'Is there any way you can call off the Clinch Mountain boys?'

'I don't know,' Ross said, sagging into his chair. 'I'm the one who called them in, but Blakely is the one who's paid them. If only the Tanglewood gang hadn't kidnapped Cole Lockhart! That complicates matters. Believe it or not, Cole is an intelligent man and not hard to deal with. He doesn't have a personal stake in this. He works for money. I could buy him off if he were here. He would rather have his pockets full of cash than risk getting half of his crew shot up. But Cole isn't here,' Ross sighed. 'The rest of the boys are unpredictable, like Leo. They might feel that there's a point of honor involved and they need to rescue Cole or be viewed as quitters. I don't know. . . .' Ross rubbed his face with the palms of both hands. 'I'll try talking to them. We'll see. I'm afraid that things may only get worse from here on, not better.'

'Is there anything else you'd like to tell me before I go?' Laredo asked.

'I suppose I'd better,' Ross who was now a defeated man answered. 'Marshal Standish is laying a trap for Dan Sumner at Gentry Cousins's house. The idea is something I proposed out of desperation. He is going to promise Dan amnesty in exchange for the location of the Tanglewood gang's camp.'

'What makes you think Sumner would turn on his friends?' Laredo asked sourly.

'Kate Cousins,' Ross answered, raising his defeated eyes to meet Laredo's.

Ross and Marshal Kaylin Standish had approached Gentry Cousins earlier. Cousins had narrowed his eyes at the sight of the crooked banker and his jaw had clamped tightly shut. He greeted them on his porch with the terse, 'Thought of something else you can do to ruin me?'

'It's not that, Gentry,' the lantern-jawed marshal said, trying to use a tone of reasonableness, something he was not good at. Kaylin Standish was not a born politician.

'We've come to offer you a way out,' Ross said. 'Out of all your troubles.'

Gentry Cousins was scowling. He didn't believe a word these two said, but there was a glimmer of hope flickering in the back of his mind. As things now stood, he was ruined and he knew it. It could do no harm at least to listen.

'You might as well come in,' Gentry said. The two men crossed the sill while a third, the bulky deputy named Jake Fromm, watched their horses. Gentry stood before the cold fireplace, hands behind his back. The others remained standing as well, facing him. 'Let's get right to it – what do you have in mind?' Gentry wanted to know.

'We have in mind letting you retain ownership of the Wabash Saloon,' Ross said. 'And getting your daughter away from those outlaws she's been riding with. That can only get worse, you know, Gentry. There will be fighting up in the Tanglewood and people hurt. Even if she doesn't get injured or killed, she'll have no course to follow except riding the outlaw trail herself.'

'I know that,' Cousins said with anger. He had brooded on it day and night for a long while – ever since Dan Sumner had been driven off his land and outlawed. 'What do you intend to do about it? What can you do!'

'We have it in mind to offer Sumner amnesty in return for giving us the location of the outlaw camp. Dan is only a kid; we want Trace Dawson and Curt Wagner before they can make more trouble than they already have,' the marshal said.

'Who knows what they have in mind to try next?' Ross pitched in.

Gentry Cousins only stared at the men for a long minute. Slowly he asked, 'You expect Dan Sumner to accept that bargain?'

'We expect you – and Kate – to talk him into it,' Ross said, speaking only a part of the truth. They had other cards to play, but Gentry did not need to know this.

'It won't work,' Gentry said heavily. He did not believe it would, and that therefore meant that his hopes for retrieving himself from this situation were faint. He was stone broke and alone without even a daughter to comfort him. 'What would you want me to do?' he asked finally.

'Just let the marshal and Jake roost here for awhile,' Ross said, trying for an encouraging smile. 'I won't be here; I wouldn't be much help. Besides, I've got a bank to run.'

When Dan and Kate had approached the house of her father, Dan Sumner carefully searched the yard and the oak grove with his eyes, looking for unfamiliar horses, for patches of color where none belonged, for the glint of sunlight off metal. He saw nothing suspicious; still he had deep forebodings about this. He understood Kate's need to reassure her father, but still this smelled like trouble. For her he would do it, however, though he might regret it later.

'What are we waiting for,' Kate Cousins asked after another minute.

'Nothing, I suppose,' Dan answered with a heavy sigh, and they started their horses toward the house.

Reaching it, they flipped the reins of their ponies over the hitch rail and started up the steps to the porch, Dan's eyes still flickering from point to point. There was a stillness in the air. No birds sang, no dog came to meet them. Something was wrong; he knew it in his bones, but they had come too far to turn around now even if Kate were willing. And she was not; there was an eagerness in her eyes as she crossed the threshold – the thrill of being home again. It lasted until Dan crossed the sill and felt a pair of bearish arms thrown around him, his revolver slipped from his holster.

Across the room he saw the sudden fear in Kate's eyes, saw a worried Gentry Cousins standing near the grandfather clock, saw Kaylin Standish, pistol in his hands, smiling nastily.

'Let him go, Jake,' the marshal said. 'We've got his teeth. He won't be trying anything.'

'What's all of this?' Dan asked although he knew.

'You're under arrest, Sumner. For bank robbery and anything else I can think of.'

Gentry looked betrayed. He had one arm around Kate's slender shoulders. 'That wasn't the bargain!' he complained.

'What bargain?' Kaylin Standish said coldly.

'Father, did you—?' Kate asked.

'This is not what I agreed to!' Gentry complained.

'The law doesn't make bargains,' Standish said coldly. To one side Jake Fromm watched, rifle in hand, his beady little eyes glittering.

'What do you want?' Dan asked, knowing that there was a game being played here. Otherwise he would already be on his way to the Lordsberg jail.

'Tell us how to find your camp in the Tanglewood,' Standish said. 'Take us there and I'll do what I can to get you a softer sentence. Otherwise you'll spend twenty or twenty-five years in the Denver prison. That's a long time, kid. I want Trace and Curt Wagner, and you're the one who can help me get them.'

'I won't do that!' Dan said heatedly. 'I never would.'

'You might as well say good-bye to Kate now, then. You'll never see her again.'

'Dan!' Kate shouted, twisting away from her father's arm. 'I can't go on if—'

'What about you, Kate?' the marshal asked. 'You know where the camp is, too. Storm Ross has said he'll return your father's saloon if one of you helps us find the Tanglewood camp. And if you refuse, you'll never see Dan again except in prison garb. A very old man in prison garb. What do you say? It's not your life I'm talking about, but the lives of the two men in this room that you care about. What do you say, Kate?'

Kate's eyes went from Dan's to her father's which remained miserably staring at the floor. She looked toward Dan again and raised both of her hands toward the ceiling.

'What am I supposed to do, Dan! I can't let you both down.' She nodded her head slowly. 'All right, Marshal—'

'Kate!' Dan shouted.

'All right, Marshal,' Kate said in a small voice, 'I'll guide you out to the Tanglewood camp.'

'Jake,' Kaylin Standish instructed his deputy, 'round up the Clinch Mountain boys. It's time for them show us what they're made of.'

CHAPTER ELEVEN

Laredo didn't like the way things were shaping up. What he needed was time – in a few weeks, perhaps a few days, the illegal chicanery of Blakely and Ross could probably be proven in court. Without further pay the Clinch Mountain boys would probably drift away toward more profitable ventures and the Wakapee Valley men could move back on to their land and start afresh. But things seem to have reached the boiling point.

As he passed through Lordsberg he saw the Clinch Mountain boys saddling their horses, preparing to ride. None of them had a bottle of whiskey in hand, none seemed to be lingering in the saloons. They were ready to go to work.

He did not know what had happened, but after what Ross had told him of their plan – Ross's and Marshal Standish's – he could make a good guess. His conviction grew stronger as he passed the marshal's office and spotted Kate Cousins's little blue roan hitched there. Somehow they had convinced her to turn traitor, probably by arresting Dan Sumner. Kate's generous impulse to ride to her father's house had been used to their advantage, and probably would turn the Tanglewood into a killing field.

Laredo rode on, just a little faster. The sun was already lowering its head behind the imposing heights of the Rocky Mountains. There weren't many hours of daylight left. That meant that the Clinch Mountain boys would be on the move soon. Laredo had little time.

His official obligations had already been fulfilled. The suspect liens, contracts and deeds had been delivered to Tucson, the stolen money returned to the bank; still he felt a moral obligation to assist the wronged Tanglewood desperadoes. His superiors at the Bank Examiner's office would think no less of him if he returned now. He had done his duty. But Laredo would think less of himself, and that mattered more.

As he rode, he considered that Dusty, too, would think less of him. Dusty, his little red-headed wife, always asked him to recount his travels. Often they would sit at the table in their small Crater, Arizona, cottage and she would lean forward, watching him eagerly, and sometimes with horror as Laredo told her what he had been through this time. She would pour them coffee and serve shoo-fly pie which only Southerners knew how to make. Dusty was from the south – of Ireland. From a town named Kilkeel. No, she would not like him to end his saga that way, although she had begged him many times to give up this line of work. Dusty had quite a bit of inherited money and tried to convince him that he didn't need to go out and risk life and limb; she had seen her man shot up and beaten before, but after he was healed, she didn't bother trying to convince him to give it up, trade in his saddle for a front porch rocking chair.

Laredo rode on, thinking all of these things – and many others concerning Dusty.

All the time the sun continued to fade slowly behind the high mountains and the shadows to grow longer. Laredo had already made his decision to help out the Tanglewood crowd if he could. He only wondered how much of a lead he had on Marshal Standish and the Clinch Mountain boys.

Laredo wove his way along the complicated trail he had followed out of the Tanglewood. Once an irate bobcat appeared in a tree beside the road, baring its fangs, hissing displeasure at his intrusion. He rounded the last bend in the trail and entered the camp, but they were gone. Nothing remained but a few burned twigs in the cold fire ring.

He pondered. It must have been because they knew of Dan Sumner's last risky ride into Lordsberg. They had been right to move on. The question was, how was Laredo to find them now? He had things to tell them, matters to discuss.

Night was settling. He listened but heard only silence, looked around but saw nothing moving. They had withdrawn into the depths of the Tanglewood. Neither friend nor foe was going to locate them easily now. There was still enough light to see by although purple dusk was settling rapidly, the land cooling quickly. There was no obvious trail leading away in the opposite direction. He could be seen – if anyone was looking his way. Laredo decided to chance it, even knowing that Trace Dawson, especially, did not trust him. He drew his revolver and fired a shot into the air.

No one called out; perhaps they did not wish to be found by him again.

Then, high up on a shadowed mountain ridge, Laredo picked out a brief flickering fire, like a match wavering in the wind – which, as it turned out, was exactly what it had been, and he started his reluctant horse in that direction. They bucked through the wildly tangled brush every bit as rough if not rougher than that of the Texas big thicket country where Laredo had once as a young man made his living working longhorn steers from the confusion of the thorny thickets. That was the country where the wearing of chaps and *tapaderos* was mandatory, and Laredo reflected that he could make good use of their protection now from the blackthorn and mesquite, the nopal cactus which seemed to flourish everywhere.

He eventually found, thought he had found, the foot of a trail leading up toward the evening-shadowed ridge where he had seen the glimmer of light earlier. His arms were thorn-cut, his pant legs studded with cactus spines. There was no point in turning back now, and so he started the faithful buckskin up the narrow, danger-ous trail, mentally apologizing to the horse.

The trail wound in and out, at times coming quite near to the edge of a precipice falling away into the darkness. There was a swarm of bats whipping past his head now, off on their night hunt for insects to devour.

Laredo swung his hat at them. He had no fondness for the tiny flying creatures. Once, on the trail near Albuquerque, he had been forced to take shelter from the weather in a bat cave where the leathery-winged things fluttered all night and their distinctive guano stink filled his nostrils and touched his throat as he tried to sleep. They were filthy little things.

Finally Laredo crested out the trail and company was there to meet him. Trace Dawson and Curt Wagner approached him. He found himself on a long bench cut into the side of the hill where a craggy nearby cave with an arched opening was still flooded with emerging bats.

'Nice neighborhood,' Laredo said, swinging down heavily from his exhausted horse. The other two didn't seem to share his disgust toward bats. Curt shrugged and answered, 'There wasn't a lot of choice.'

'I suppose not,' Laredo replied.

'What did you come back for?' Trace demanded. The man's temper was getting shorter as the days passed. Then Laredo let his eyes stray and he thought he saw the reason behind it. Ruby stood to one side, deep in shadows, her hair loose around her shoulders. The man was deeply concerned for her, Laredo guessed. He had every right to be.

'They're coming,' Laredo told them. 'The Clinch Mountain boys are riding this way.'

'Tonight?' Curt said with disbelief. He glanced at the sundown skies. 'At this time of day?'

'I think they worked out this would be a good time to come down at you as you settled in for the night. They

131

know where the old camp is.'

'How could they?' Trace asked in bewilderment.

'If you'll let me talk, I'll try to explain things,' Laredo said.

And he did, telling them about the trap laid for Dan Sumner in Lordsberg.

'That wouldn't be enough to make Dan turn yellow,' Trace said with certainty.

'No, but I think they brought enough pressure on Kate Cousins to make her reveal all she knows.'

'What do you suggest?' Curt asked Laredo.

'I was going to say that you should just cut Cole Lockhart loose,' Laredo said, nodding toward the two prisoners who sat together leaning against the wall of the bluff, their hands as well as their feet now bound.

'Why him?' asked Prince Blakely, who had been listening.

'Because, Blakely, there will be no more money forthcoming from Ross. Even if Ross didn't take my warning seriously, within a few days all of the bank's funds will be frozen until the books can be gone over thoroughly. With no more pay, the Clinch Mountain boys will eventually just fade away. They're only here now, I suspect, to rescue Cole.

'Of course,' Laredo went on. 'The risk is too great now. Cole knows where your new camp is situated. You can't let him go, I'm afraid.'

'Then what can we do?' Trace asked.

'Fort up, boys, you're in for a fight.'

At the last moment Dan had relented. He refused to let

Kate Cousins ride off in the company of the rough Clinch Mountain boys, and he agreed after a struggle with his jumbled emotions to lead the gang of killers to the camp of the Tanglewood Desperadoes. It was him or Kate, and that was no choice. They had left him none.

The burly man, the one he had heard called Leo, rode beside him so closely that their horses frequently bumped shoulders as the sun died in the west and the high mountains blushed purple in the dusk light. The Tanglewood, below them, was black as a pit.

'Down there?' Dan heard one of the other riders exclaim, observing the close, thorny growth in the wild country beyond the trail. No one answered the astonished man. The others were determined, grim-faced. They were rugged men, accustomed to a rugged way of life.

Marshal Standish who had come along, accompanied by his deputies, Jake and Marvin, not willing to miss out on the glory, was silent for the most part. Now, as they started down the winding trail, he asked Dan Sumner, 'Are you sure this is the way?'

'It always has been,' Dan answered. His voice was brittle. There was an edge to it; he had been forced into doing something he had sworn that he would never do. He was now a traitor as well. No better than Johnny Johnson, worse in fact – Johnny had taken their money, but Dan was about to give his brothers-in-arms over to these killers.

'I don't see anything,' Leo groused after another half-mile.

133

Neither did Dan, and as they rounded the last bend in the trail and emerged where the camp had been, he saw why.

'They've pulled up stakes,' he said to the dozen or so hard men around him. There was nothing there but a few charred sticks in the fire ring and many horse tracks to indicate that this had been the camp of the Tanglewood outlaws.

'Why would they do that?' Marshal Standish demanded as their heads were surrounded by hungry mosquitoes and other flying pests.

'Well, I guess they didn't trust me to keep a secret,' Dan said. And they had been right not to.

'Where would they go?' Leo asked, swatting at the insects, looking around the tangled vastness.

'I don't know,' Dan said honestly.

'We can pick up their trail,' Jake said hopefully, but no one gave that suggestion much credence. Through the network of brush at this hour of the day, the idea seemed ridiculous.

'We'd be riding blind into their gunsights,' Leo said. 'We can't see them, but I'll bet they have a spot where they can see us coming.'

'They have to have headed for high ground,' Marshal Standish concluded and his eyes lifted to the bench along the face of the hills, his vision drawn there by the clouds of bats now issuing forth from the cavern in huge swarms, seeking their evening meal. 'They're up there,' he said confidently, pointing toward the ledge. 'I would be.'

'What do you think, Leo?' one of the Clinch

Mountain boys asked.

'I think he's right,' Leo said. 'The question is, how do we get up there, and how do we attack them? They're bound to see twenty mounted men crashing through the brush.'

'Cole is up there with them, unless they've killed him. We've got to make a try. I can't tell you how many times Cole Lockhart has pulled me out of tight scrapes,' said another of the gang.

'How many men are up there?' Leo wanted to know, looking from Dan to Kaylin Standish.

'Well. There's Trace Dawson and Curt Wagner, of course,' Standish answered, scratching at his cheek where he had been bitten by a mosquito. 'Probably this – what's his name, Dan? The stranger?'

'Laredo, he calls himself.'

'And I've heard there might be as many as twenty more.'

'But you've never seen them?'

'No,' Standish admitted.

'I think that there's only two or three men up there,' Leo concluded, looking toward the overhang where the bats continued to swarm. 'The rest was pure bluff.'

'What do you want to do, Leo?' a Clinch Mountain man asked as the sky settled to a darker purple.

'Get up there and cut Cole loose. He's done as much for me as he has for any of you. Let's find a trail, boys, and if we can't find one, we'll make one!'

'They're coming, Trace,' Curt Wagner said, nudging Dawson from a half-doze.

'Of course they are,' Cole Lockhart said. 'I know my men – they wouldn't desert me. If you had any sense you'd just set me free now. I can call them off.'

'But would you?' Trace asked. Cole had already made his threats and he trusted the leader of the Clinch Mountain boys about as far as he would a diamondback rattlesnake. Cole didn't bother to answer.

'What about me?' they heard Prince Blakely ask Lockhart. It still hadn't fully occurred to Blakely that he was a man of no further importance or use to anyone involved.

'Better figure where you're going to set up,' Laredo suggested. The sounds of horses crashing through the brush below them had grown nearer. It would be dark soon and the Clinch Mountain boys would want to make their assault while there was still enough light to shoot by.

'I guess we'd better,' Curt agreed. 'It's either that or withdraw further.' But looking up the hillslope, he could see there was no place else to go. They had managed to box themselves in. The bench had seemed ideal at the time, but now without the option of escape, it could prove to be a death trap.

It all depended on how eager the Clinch Mountain boys were to draw blood.

Plenty eager, it seemed, as the first of the horsemen below emerged from the heavy brush and arrived at a small dry-grass clearing at the foot of the bluff. How they hoped to charge the hill successfully was not evident; that was probably why their leaders had held up – to devise a strategy.

The poor light was going to hinder them, certainly, but Laredo knew that there were two narrow trails leading up to the bluff and only three men to hold them.

'Last chance,' Cole Lockhart said.

'Or I could just hand you my gun and let you shoot me,' Trace said with bitter anger. 'Ruby, get as far back as you can.'

'I *can* shoot, you know,' Ruby said defiantly.

'I know you can – I just don't want you doing it. Get back, even if it means hiding in the cave.'

'With those bats!'

'They're nasty, but not deadly,' Trace snapped, obviously now uneasy not for his own safety, but for Ruby Lee's.

'Better pick your positions,' Laredo repeated. 'I'll set up to watch the south trail. I doubt they'll find it in this light, but you never know. We can't be having them walk in the back door.'

Laredo started in that direction, Winchester in hand, wondering why he had volunteered himself for this fight which should have been none of his own. He found a good position – a huge split yellow boulder with a notch for firing. It nearly faced the trail head. It would be difficult for anyone to get past his rifle until darkness settled. Then he would not be able to see anyone approaching. Convincing himself that it would be equally difficult for anyone to follow the narrow trail in full darkness, he settled in to wait.

Just as the first shots rang out, echoing across the Tanglewood.

CHAPTER TWELVE

The first Clinch Mountain man that Curt Wagner saw must have been half-Indian. He had managed to slip through the shadows halfway up the north trail before anyone heard or saw him coming. But the man rose up and was silhouetted against the stars, illuminated faintly by the light of smoky dusk and Curt settled his sights on him and triggered off. The man waved his hands wildly in the air and then toppled from the trail to plunge to the earth fifty feet below.

One down, twenty to go.

After trying the sneak assault, the Clinch Mountain boys adopted more muscular tactics. Curt had given notice that he was there, but had also given his position away and a barrage of rifle fire peppered the rocks where he had taken shelter. They must have fired fifty, a hundred bullets in his direction, spraying him with rock chips as the lead ricocheted off into the cool night, singing past his head.

Curt hunkered down, covering his head. There was nothing else he could do without taking a few bullets.

Across the way Trace opened up with his rifle, scattering a few of the Clinch Mountain boys. That just succeeded in bring a fusillade of shots in his direction and Trace found himself forced to take cover as well. They were simply outgunned. The Clinch Mountain boys were determined to rescue Cole. Maybe, Trace thought, they should have considered Cole's offer more seriously.

The Clinch Mountain boys certainly were not lacking ammunition. Shots rang out constantly, and there was no way for Curt or Trace even to lift their heads, let alone draw a bead. Both men knew what the idea behind this was; there would be men ascending the trail by now, protected by covering fire. Sooner or later there would be no choice but to rise up and face the music. Trace hoped that Ruby had followed his advice and retreated to the shelter of the cave, although there was no guarantee of real safety there since Cole, obviously, knew where she was. There was no telling what the outlaw leader would plan for her if his men were victorious.

Laredo watched the heavy fighting from his position above the south trail. No one had so far tried to approach the camp on that side of the bluff. Possibly, as he had speculated, no one knew of its existence. Still you never knew. He considered firing back from his shelter, to try to help the two men out, but that would be advertising his own position. Maybe it was better to wait things out. If any of the Clinch Mountain boys achieved the bench, that would be the time to cut loose. For now he would hold his fire as a storm of bullets pierced the night. Laredo saw one wildly aimed shot take down a bat in flight. It would have been comic – under the circumstances.

The guns below fell silent. To Laredo that meant only one thing – the Clinch Mountain boys figured that they had achieved their goal and were now in position to rush the ledge. Further fire would come too close to their own men as they assaulted the camp. Feeling now that the south trail would not be utilized in the attack, he slipped away from the boulders and made his way back toward Curt and Trace, moving in a low crouch.

He had taken no more than a dozen steps when he saw one of the raiders hoist himself up over the lip of the bench and begin moving stealthily toward Curt Wagner's position, pistol in hand.

'Hey!' Laredo called out, not too loudly, and the man turned toward him, gun lifting. As he swung toward Laredo, Laredo shot him. The bullet from his Winchester caught the Clinch Mountain man full in the chest and he staggered back, falling over the rim of the bluff.

That had been only a sample of what was to be. Before Laredo could reach Curt where he knelt positioned behind a stack of broken rocks, the assault began in earnest. In the light of purple dusk maybe half a dozen or a dozen dark shadows emerged from the head of the north trail, crawled up on to the bench and began their eerie, starlit attack.

Laredo shot one man, switched his sights to another without pausing to see how much damage his bullet had done, and continued firing at the silhouetted raiders who seemed to have little more substance than arcade targets – except they were firing back.

Laredo slumped behind the rocks, fishing for more shells for his Winchester as Curt banged away with his own rifle. Across the way Laredo saw a man creeping up on Trace Dawson's position, Colt in hand, and he yelled out a warning. Trace spun and fired, catching the man in the abdomen with a shot from his rifle.

The evening grew still.

'Think they've had enough?' Curt Wagner asked in a dry voice.

'There's no telling. They may just be regrouping.'

'How many of them did we get?'

Laredo just shook his head. He couldn't estimate. Maybe three or four, perhaps half a dozen. Half their force? There was no telling. He did have a suggestion.

'Maybe we ought to pull back, Curt.'

'To where? There's nowhere to go.'

'The cave. That way there's no way anyone can get behind us. They'll play hell digging us out of there.'

'It's a filthy place,' Curt said with disgust. 'Centuries of bat guano.'

'You couldn't hate those flying vennin as much as I do,' Laredo answered, 'but it's the safest refuge we have available.'

'I suppose you're right,' Curt said with a heavy sigh. 'Tell Trace – he's still the man in charge.'

Trace seemed more willing than either Laredo or Curt to pull back to the cave. Ruby would be there. 'The prisoners?' was all he asked Laredo.

'We'll drag them along. They might still prove to be bargaining chips, used properly.'

A few more of the Clinch Mountain boys had made it up on to the bench and shots rang out as they fired at the retreating men. Laredo fired back at the muzzle flashes as Trace and Curt hurried the prisoners on toward the shelter of the cave. Someone yelled out and the Clinch Mountain gang now held their fire. They must have realized that Cole Lockhart was among the fleeing men and were afraid of tagging their leader with a stray bullet.

They would hold off for a time now to reassess their position, but they would come forward again eventually. They weren't accustomed to losing battles, and they weren't prepared to accept defeat.

Complete darkness settled as the three Tanglewood men – Laredo was beginning to consider himself one of them – sheltered up in the cave leaving their prisoners seated against the front wall. The stench in the cave was almost unbearable to Laredo. Inches thick everywhere across the floor of the cave, mounded in favorite roosting places, the guano stank like decomposing bodies drenched in ammonia. He kept as near to the mouth of the cave as possible.

The smell was so reminiscent of that gun battle in an Albuquerque cave, that it carried a memory of death with it to his deepest senses. He smiled grimly. Like everything else in his life, these events seemed never to end, just to become cyclical, recurring at the whims of Fate.

It was at times like this that he thought Dusty was right: he should get out of this business.

'See any of them?' Curt asked at his shoulder and

142

Laredo shook his head.

'We're not likely to in this light. Unless someone makes a clumsy mistake.

'I can still get you out of this,' Cole Lockhart said from his seated position along the streaked wall.

'Maybe we should at least consider the offer,' Curt said.

'Are you crazy?' Trace Dawson said. 'All we'd accomplish is giving the enemy one more gunhand. He's not the sort of man you can trust.'

'I can get the bar girl out of this alive,' Cole said, nodding toward Ruby who was only a shadow in the cave.

'Trace?'

'No,' Dawson said firmly.

'What do you think, Laredo?' Curt Wagner asked.

'If I have a vote,' Laredo said, 'I'm with Trace on this – you'd be making a deal with the devil.'

'You're right, of course,' Wagner the former lawman, said heavily. Glancing around he commented, 'It's just that I never thought I'd have to end my days in a place like this. I was grasping at straws.'

'Let's put our heads together and try to find another solution,' Laredo said. 'The Clinch Mountain boys aren't planning on peppering the cave with fire or they would have begun already. I suppose they don't want to risk hitting Lockhart, which they might with the way bullets would ricochet around in here.'

'What then?' Curt asked. The tall man looked older now, his face strained and drawn. 'We can't rush them and we can't escape.'

'Maybe we can,' Ruby said, walking toward them.

'What do you mean?' Trace asked her.

'Hasn't anyone noticed? It's lighter in here than it has a right to be, and I've seen a few bats enter the cave from somewhere other than that opening. There's another way in – and out – somewhere.'

'Large enough for a bat,' Curt said.

'And maybe for us. Let's at least look,' she said, encouraging the men.

Curt, who had no faith in the plan, was left to stand watch at the mouth of the cave while Trace and Laredo followed Ruby Lee to where she had seen what might have been an opening in the roof. She pointed up, but neither man saw anything.

Until Laredo spotted a clearly shining star glimmering in a small gap in the cavern ceiling. He nudged Trace and pointed it out. The roof was low enough that a man could reach it jumping up. It was a small aperture, no more than three feet wide, but it was a possible exit.

'What would we do even if we could get up there?' Trace asked pessimistically.

'What are we going to do here?' Laredo said. 'I say we give it a try.'

'So do I,' Ruby agreed. 'Trace,' she said, taking his hand, 'it's a hope. Staying here is only slow suicide.'

'The prisoners would have to be untied. . . .'

'To hell with the prisoners,' Laredo said with heat. 'Leave them here. Cole's men will eventually come to rescue him – as to what happens to Blakely, do we really care?'

'It's a chance, Trace,' Ruby said, and there was enough starlight to show the pleading in her eyes. It was that more than anything that had been said that made Trace Dawson decide.

'All right then. Let's see if we can wriggle through. Curt!' he called, 'can you hold them back?'

'I can try. I don't see anyone moving yet.'

Trace nodded, looking up at the narrow opening. 'All right; who goes first?'

'I'll try it if you'll give me a leg up,' Laredo volunteered. At least if he died it would be in the fresh air. There could be men up there watching, but that seemed unlikely. No one without leathery wings had explored this cave for centuries. Who would want to?

Trace handed Ruby his rifle and clasped his hands together, forming a boosting strap for Laredo. Laredo reached out, grasped the rim of the opening and pulled down a shower of rocks and mud left from the rain of the day before. He bowed his head and sputtered but remained where he was, reaching up again. This time he found firm purchase and with Trace Dawson hoisting from below, Laredo clambered up and out, rolling on to his stomach on the firm ground above, which proved to be a little knoll with scattered sagebrush and a small stand of nopal cactus.

Laredo peered down into the hole and gestured, then he crawled forward to look down along the bench where he could see the Clinch Mountain boys taking up their positions behind the rocks, apparently intent on waiting out the cornered Tanglewood gang, at least until morning light. Laredo crept back to the opening and gestured with his hand.

Ruby was the next one up. Laredo motioned for her to be silent.

Curt, seeing what was going on, had taken the time to gag their two prisoners with his scarf and Cole's own bandana. They could not risk having an alarm raised now. Then he crossed to the ceiling opening where still small rocks and mud trickled into the cave, formed a stirrup for Trace and hoisted him up. Curt was last, but he was several inches taller than the other men and he was able simply to leap up and grip the rim of the opening. Laredo's hand shot down and grabbed his belt, helping Curt up and over the edge.

None of them had an idea where they were, or which way to go, but communicating in sign language, they decided to strike out toward the north, across the knoll, leaving the bats to their home.

A chill had settled again and clouds appeared to the north. The scent of sagebrush was heavy in the air, and they traveled on only by starlight, it being too early for the moon. More than once Laredo stumbled, tripping over rocks and unseen chaparral plants, but he was breathing clean air away from the stench of the cave and he actually smiled in the darkness. If everything was truly cyclical, and he had escaped a cave again, then that meant that he was destined to arrive home safely again to his Dusty.

CHAPTER THIRTEEN

There must have been a dozen people inside Storm Ross's Lordsberg bank when Laredo ambled in the next morning at sunrise after a rough trek across the countryside. The town mayor was there along with three men Laredo knew well from the Tucson Bank Examiner's office, a couple of legal men along with a US marshal from Denver who had arrived on the evening stage, and Laredo's boss, Deacon Cody, himself.

'Well, Laredo, things do get tangled up, don't they?' Deacon said, taking Laredo's hand warmly.

'It seems so. Why am I the one who always gets these kinds of cases.'

Deacon Cody was not smiling when he replied, 'Because you're the best, Laredo. That's all there is to it. How much time are you going to want off?'

'Enough to reacquaint myself with my wife anyway – a month probably. I'll be getting antsy and ready to go again by then, I'd guess.'

'Well, I suppose we can spare you for that long,'

Deacon said, looping his arm over Laredo's shoulders, 'although we have been having trouble with a string of bank robberies down in the Mesa area. . . .'

'I'll talk to you about it later,' Laredo said. 'What's going on here?'

'What isn't? I've seen dirtier banks before, but I can't remember when. The men from Denver are going over the books. As of now they've already determined that the lands seized from the displaced Wakapee Valley were taken illegally – the reason he's been sent down here,' Deacon said, nodding at the big redheaded man with the US marshal's badge on his vest. 'Someone is going to prison, that's for sure.'

'And the Tanglewood gang?' Laredo asked carefully.

'Why, they'll get their land back of course.'

'I meant . . . criminal charges?'

'Who's going to file them?' Deacon asked reasonably. 'Not the bank, not the town marshal who has not yet returned from the Tanglewood, as you call it, and probably got himself shot up there. Not the mayor – he's over there, and just told me that he wants a decent man as Lordsberg's marshal and has hired someone named Curt Wagner again, if you know him.'

Laredo only nodded. He was weary beyond words. Deacon Cody could see that now, and he quit talking except to say, 'Go home, Laredo. Report to me in thirty days.'

'I will,' he promised, 'unless I come up with enough common sense in the meantime to take Dusty's advice and finally get out of this business.'

'There's another minor matter,' Deacon said, just as

Curt Wagner, wearing a badge on his shirt front, entered the bank from the sun bright street. 'But I'll let the town marshal ask you.'

'How are you doing?' Curt asked, taking Laredo's hand warmly.

'Tired, that's all.'

'So am I – all of us – but having this returned,' he said, tapping his badge, 'has given me fresh energy. I suppose I'll collapse on my bed tonight, but for now, I'm enjoying everything. We've got Ross, Blakely and Judge Weems sitting in jail, waiting for transport to Denver if the examiners find enough evidence to prosecute, which I'm told they already have. I passed by the Wabash Saloon on my way over and saw Gentry Cousins sweeping off the porch. He told me that Dan Sumner and Kate had stopped at the preacher's and were now on their way out to his ranch. No one's seen Trace; I think he's sleeping the day away up in Ruby's room.'

'Smart man,' Laredo said, yawning.

'This is all happening fast – thanks to you, Laredo.'

'Me? You're the ones who began the fight, stood up for yourselves. I just happened by.'

'Maybe. I don't see it that way. The only other matter is your horse. When Blakely escaped he was trying to ride to his house on your buckskin. So I guess technically he could be tried as a horse thief if you cared to make a complaint.'

'The man's got enough problems,' Laredo said, yawning again, 'and I don't feel up to it. Did you see my horse? What kind of shape was it in?'

'It looked fine to me and it's been over at the stable

eating and resting for awhile, so I suppose he's trail-ready. Why, are you planning on going home?'

'Am I not!' Laredo said. 'It's nothing against the people of Lordsberg or of Wakapee Valley, but I've seen all I need to see of it.'

'I understand,' Curt said, shaking Laredo's hand again.

'Is that all of it?' Laredo asked Deacon Cody.

'Just about. Cole Lockhart escaped with about half of his crew. He'll pop up again sometime, I know, but for now he's taken cover somewhere.' Deacon hesitated, 'You sure you aren't up to looking into those bank robberies down around Mesa?'

'I'm sure!' Laredo exclaimed. 'Send another of your hired lunatics out there.'

Deacon laughed, also shook Laredo's hand and watched as he strode out the door, saying to Curt Wagner, 'He's the best I've ever seen. At least the best man I have.'

'I wouldn't want him on my trail,' Curt agreed. Then, shifting his gun in its holster, he told the others, 'I'd better get out there and start patrolling my town.' There was a slight emphasis on the word 'my' and Deacon Cody smiled faintly as the tall man swaggered from the bank. Then Deacon turned back to confer further with his legal people who had been finding fraudulent entry after fraudulent entry in the bank's ledgers.

By the time Laredo cleared the town line he was bone tired. He should have stayed over another night, but he needed to get home. By the time he made Arizona he recognized the fact that he had to stop somewhere. He had fallen asleep in the saddle and been jolted awake by a misstep of the buckskin horse. He had driven the horse too hard. Despite its earlier rest, it was obviously being pushed to its limit, and that wasn't fair to the faithful animal.

'We'll halt at Los Coches,' Laredo told the horse, patting its neck. 'I've had enough, too.'

The little pueblo, mostly of adobe block structures, small and squat, rested along a tiny till surrounded by a scattering of oak trees. The residents had little to support themselves with, but they had been there for generations and so here they stayed.

Laredo aimed his pony toward the La Paloma Restaurant where Maria had always welcomed him when he happened to be passing through. A stout, hearty woman with few teeth, she was prone to embrace Laredo and make him special meals with her own hands. How he had charmed her in the first place, he could not remember, but she treated him like a long-lost son.

Swinging down from the shuddering buckskin as sunset began to streak the sky with color, Laredo entered the restaurant.

The first person he saw was Johnny Johnson.

Johnny was wearing a white apron with food stains on it. He smiled sheepishly, but genuinely as he saw Laredo enter the cool, dark interior of the restaurant. He walked toward him a little warily.

'Hello, Johnny,' Laredo said.

'I guess you're surprised to find that I'm still here.'

'Yes, as a matter of fact.'

Johnny guided Laredo to a booth in the corner where a roughly-made bench provided the seating. Johnny sat opposite him. Beyond in the kitchen something spicy was being prepared – *tamales*, Laredo thought, his stomach growled.

'You sent me down here, and I told Maria that you were a friend of mine. I mentioned that I was going to spend the night in the stable, and she would have none of it. She said I was to sleep on a cot in her back room. Then she fed me! Did she feed me! When I was stuffed, I placed the twenty-dollar gold piece you loaned me on the table and she lifted her hands as if horrified. "No, no, no," she kept saying, then she backed away and left. I had a minute or two to talk to her in the morning and told her that I really had no place to go and she asked me if I wanted to work here for a while. I didn't, not really, but it's been fine.'

'I've good news for you, Johnny,' Laredo informed him. 'You've got your ranch back.'

Johnny didn't seem as excited by the news as Laredo had expected. Then, looking past Johnny's shoulder, Laredo saw the kitchen door open and caught a glimpse of a tiny sloe-eyed girl peeking out. She was Johnny's age, around eighteen or nineteen years old, and Laredo thought he had matters figured.

'What's her name?' he asked Johnny Johnson.

'Who?' Johnny spun to look, but the girl had ducked away. 'It's Esmerelda,' he said with a sort of dumb look on his face. 'Maria's niece.'

'Cute little thing.'

'Isn't she?' Johnny said, growing more animated. It was obvious now why he had chosen to remain here, working in a restaurant.

'She might like to have a place of her own,' Laredo suggested.

'Do you think so, Laredo? Things haven't gotten that far between us yet, but she might like my ranch on the Wakapee, don't you think?'

'A lot of women would.'

'I wonder – do you think I should ask her?'

'That's up to you. But these are Spanish people, Johnny. Before you do anything, you should talk to her parents. That's the way things are done.'

'She doesn't have any parents,' Johnny said. 'Killed by Apaches years ago. She's only got her Aunt, Maria.'

'Well, then—' At that moment, Maria burst from the kitchen, her arms outstretched, her toothless face grinning broadly. Flushed with pleasure, she approached the table and as Laredo stood she embraced him tightly, welcoming him effusively.

'Esmerelda,' she shouted, 'bring food for this hungry long-riding man!' To Laredo, 'I have just now made fresh batch of *tamales* with pig – what do you say?'

'Pork?' Laredo suggested.

'With pork meat. Let me see you eat!' She patted his shoulders with her thick, stubby hands. 'We have to get some meat on your bones. Where is Dusty?' she asked, glancing around.

'I've been working, Maria. You know she can't ride with me when I'm working.'

'Oh, you work too hard, Laredo,' she said, rolling the 'r' in his name.

'So do you,' he replied, seating himself again before she could get him into another rib-crushing clinch.

'Yes, I do – but I like it, Laredo. I like to give a hungry man good food. I enjoy the look on their faces when they finish and compliment me on what I have done for them, and knowing that it *was* good.'

'You should marry again, Maria,' Laredo said. Her first husband had been trampled in a cattle stampede when he was only twenty-five.

'Oh, I don't think so, Laredo! I know men, they want so many things. The one thing I know I can still give them is good food in their stomachs.'

'I think I understand.'

'I will bring you the *tamales y frijoles* and maybe a mug of cold *cerveza*,' Maria said. 'Is there anything else you want?'

'Not for me,' Laredo answered. 'But Johnny might like to have a word with you,' he added, nodding at the young man across the table. 'You might not know it but he is a well-to-do rancher over in Colorado. And now he has gotten his land back.'

'He wants to talk to me about that?' Maria said, confused by the drift of the conversation. Then Esmerelda arrived at the table, carrying a platter of hot food for Laredo. No one could miss the glance that passed between the two young people. 'Oh,' Maria said. 'He can talk to me anytime he wishes. I think I must put my "Help Wanted" sign back in the window.'

After she had bustled away, Johnny paused long

enough to say, 'Thanks, Laredo.'

'Just take good care of her, if she does say yes.'

'Oh I will!' Johnny promised. 'And she will,' he added confidently.

Laredo ate his hot, spicy food with deep enjoyment. A kid who seemed to have nothing else to do wandered past and Laredo gave him fifty cents to take his buck-skin to the nearest stable. Finishing his meal, Laredo leaned back, his stomach full, his eye lids growing heavy. A few local people had wandered in and they sat talking, laughing together. Maria had returned just as Laredo was ready to walk to the stable, close his eyes and sleep there.

'I made up a bed fresh for you,' she said. 'You must sleep here. You can have my *huevos rancheros* for break-fast in the morning and then be on your way back to Dusty.'

It was an offer he could not refuse, and he rose wearily to his feet. Patting Maria on the shoulder he said, 'It's good to have friends.'

There were four small rooms in back of the kitchen as Laredo knew from previous visits. None of them was much wider than the beds installed there. There were no other furnishings. Laredo needed none. He almost managed to put his head down on the pillow before he fell asleep.

If it hadn't been for the clatter of dishes and utensils in the kitchen beyond his wall, Laredo thought he might have slept the day away. Instead he climbed out of bed, stamped into his boots, wiped back his hair, planted his hat and went out into the corridor which was bright, the sunlight beaming through an open rear door. Maria did not seem to be around, but he was served a hearty breakfast. Finished, he slid a ten-dollar gold piece under his plate, knowing that if Maria saw it she would refuse payment for what she had provided.

He did not stop to say goodbye to her, nor to seek out Johnny. He decided that he was tired of saying goodbye to people. He only wanted to say hello to Dusty. With that in mind he tramped across the sun-bleached street of the small pueblo toward the stable which lay beyond the central plaza, where the local women washed their clothes in the public fountain amid much gossip and general laughter.

Entering the stable, he blinked, trying to adjust his eyes. No one seemed to be around. Finally, spying his buckskin horse at the end of the ranks of stalls, he started that way.

Cole Lockhart stepped out of the shadows to meet him.

CHAPTER FOURTEEN

'I've been waiting for you,' the outlaw chief said coldly.

'Why?' Laredo asked, glancing around to make sure there were no other men lurking in the shadows of the barn.

'You have to ask me that! Before you came along everything was under control. We had those Tanglewood men on the run. In fact, there were only two of them left. Along with a couple of scared women. Ross was running the bank; Blakely was running Ross. We had a big payday coming up when the job was finished. We had the local law in our hip pocket and Lordsberg belonged to us. You ruined all of that, Laredo. And you managed to get eight of my men shot up in the meantime. You ask me "why"?'

'I asked you why you were waiting for me,' Laredo said, shifting his weight slightly as his hand settled near the grips of his stag-handled Colt. 'There's nothing to be gained now by shooting me.'

'There is – pure satisfaction,' Cole said.

'Where's the rest of your gang?' Laredo wondered.

'Pretty much scattered. They didn't seem to want to follow my orders anymore. They seemed to believe that I wasn't that great a general.'

So that was it. Cole Lockhart not only believed that Laredo was the cause of him missing out on a big payday, but of humiliating him in front of the Clinch Mountain boys. Laredo was thinking that people were giving him too much credit. He had been only a small cog in the events that had brought Cole Lockhart down.

'Look, Lockhart—' Laredo began reasonably.

'*You* look,' Cole Lockhart screamed as his hand darted down toward his holstered revolver.

Laredo had been waiting for that; Cole Lockhart had given him enough warning. Laredo crouched, drawing his stag-handled Colt with practiced ease and swiftness. Lockhart's shot, fired at what he assumed to be an unmoving target sailed over Laredo's head and banged against the adobe wall of the stable, the shot leaving a roaring echo in its wake.

Laredo triggered off twice from his crouch. The first bullet might have tagged nothing, but the second shot took Cole Lockhart full in the chest and he staggered back to be drawn up short by a stall partition. As the rank of wild-eyed horses watched, Cole slid down the partition, his gun falling away from his hand, to end up seated, quite dead.

There was an uproar behind Laredo as a crowd of curious townspeople, drawn by the shots, swarmed through the stable doors. Laredo snatched up his saddle and rigged his buckskin horse. He walked it past the gathered people and swung into the saddle in the bright sunlight beyond.

The spicy meals that Maria had served him had gone down well and satisfied his hunger, but he had a sudden, strong yearning for a sweet dessert to finish them off. A large wedge of Dusty's shoo-fly pie was what he had in his mind as he trailed out of the small pueblo, heading home.

AUTHOR'S NOTE

For those readers who do not know and might be curious, 'shoo-fly pie' is a rich traditional dessert dish in the American South, whose chief ingredients are molasses, brown sugar and butter served in a baked pie shell. Often added are raisins, walnuts or pecans (Dusty's recipe).

As to how it got its name, your guess is as good as mine.